LADY JUSTICE

GETS LEI'D

LADY JUSTICE

GETS LEI'D

A WALT WILLIAMS
MYSTERY/COMEDY NOVEL

ROBERT THORNHILL

TATE PUBLISHING & Enterprises

Published by Tate Publishing & Enterprises, LLC
127 E. Trade Center Terrace | Mustang, Oklahoma 73064 USA
1.888.361.9473 | www.tatepublishing.com

Tate Publishing is committed to excellence in the publishing industry. The company reflects the philosophy established by the founders, based on Psalm 68:11,
"The Lord gave the word and great was the company of those who published it."

Published in the United States of America

ISBN: 978-1-61777-116-3
1. Fiction, Humorous
2. Fiction, Mystery & Detective, General
10.01.03

DEDICATION

To all of our wonderful friends on the beautiful
Hawaiian Islands who made our five years
there an experience we will never forget.

A hui hou kakou. Until we meet again.

PROLOGUE

When I was a little dude, maybe five or six years old, my grandma would say, "Walter, act your age!" Then she would give me "the look." At that point in my life, I had begun to grasp the concept of right and wrong, and her admonition was usually brought on by a momentary lapse into more childish behavior.

As a young teen, I was fully aware of the boundaries of proper decorum but tended to test those boundaries on occasion. These forays into inappropriate behavior were most often cut short by Mom's stern, "Walter, act your age!"

Grandma taught her well.

Now I am faced with a dilemma. Is there a point in one's life where the restraints of "acting your age" no longer apply?

If the answer is yes, then I'm home free.

If the answer is no, then someone tell me, please, how is a sixty-seven-year-old man supposed to act?

As I reflect on the events of the past year and a half, I think I started off on the right foot.

At age sixty-five, after thirty years as a real estate salesperson and landlord,

I retired and applied for Social Security. Isn't that what you're supposed to do?

But something didn't feel quite right. I was bored. My life had no direction. I began to wonder if I was through with all that life had to offer.

Then one day I witnessed the mugging of an elderly lady, and everything changed. A new fire was kindled in my bosom, and I knew the rocking chair would just have to wait.

Justice is depicted as a lady with a blindfold trying to balance the scales of life, and I knew I needed to give the blind lady a helping hand.

At the ripe old age of sixty-five, I wanted to be a cop!

Age appropriate? Who knows? But Mom and Grandma aren't around anymore, and no one stepped up and shouted, "Walter, act your age!"

As I began my new career, there were many who questioned my sanity, and I have to admit that I harbored some doubts of my own. Thankfully, I have a mentor and good friend, eighty-six-year-old Professor Leopold Skinner, my old philosophy professor from UMKC, who now is a tenant in my three-story apartment building. He helped put things into the proper perspective when he reminded me that Grandma Moses started painting in her seventies, Laura Ingalls Wilder started her *Little House on the Prairie* series in her sixties, Paul Newman didn't start racing cars until he was an old dude, and Colonel Sanders started KFC when he was in his sixties.

That was good enough for me. If the colonel could do it, so could I.

But a cop?

Come on. It's one thing to throw some secret herbs and spices in a bowl and dip a chicken. They don't fight back.

It's a whole different story when you're chasing a Latino gangbanger or a goomba from the Italian mob. They have guns!

In the year that I've been on Lady Justice's payroll, I've been poked, punched, kidnapped, shot at, and at least three times I have been close enough to death to see the bright light and smell the carnations.

And if this wasn't sufficient evidence to question my sanity, consider the fact that somehow I have become the undercover expert in our squad.

I've been a "John" in a strip bar, half of a gay couple, and donned a dress and wig, all in the name of justice. But most improbable of all, imagine a sixty-six-year-old Elvis impersonator performing live in front of 19,000 people in the Sprint Center Arena.

Each time I look around and hope someone will step up and say, "Walter, act your age!"

Instead, I see the faces of my captain, Dwayne "Shorty" Short; Ox, my partner; Vince, my first recruit in the City Retiree Action Patrol; and of all my fellow officers in the squad. And I hear their words of encouragement and congratulations for a job well done.

I see the love and admiration of my friends, Mary, Willie, and Jerry, whom I have inadvertently drug into my liaison with Lady Justice. They are my family.

But most importantly, I see Maggie McBride, my sweetie, soul mate, and bride-to-be. You see, at age sixty-seven, I will be getting married for the first time.

Am I acting my age? Heck, I don't know. I've never been this age before.

Anyway, what does age have to do with it? I recall a quote from Satchel Paige, who pitched major league baseball till age fifty-nine: "How old would you be if you didn't know how old you was?"

That's good enough for me.

Am I acting my age?

Probably not!

But I don't give a rat's ass. I'm having the time of my life.

I'm Walter Williams, and I'm a cop!

CHAPTER ONE

We are all creatures of habit. I think the Big Guy intended it that way.

The advantage is that the mundane things we do over and over again each day become hard-wired into our brains and become automatic. That frees our minds to pursue more noble and worthwhile challenges.

The downside is that once the minutiae of life become ingrained, they are awfully hard to change.

I sit at my breakfast table with my coffee and newspaper, and I swear, I can't remember how I got here.

With great difficulty, I retrace my activities from the first screech of the alarm clock to the present, and I discover that what I did is what I have done every morning for the last thirty years.

I awake with a start, slap the alarm clock, stumble into the bathroom to pee, shuffle into the kitchen, start the coffee, shuffle back for a hot shower, dress, get the newspaper, pour a cup of coffee and a bowl of Wheaties—the breakfast of champions—and read the paper while I eat.

I don't even think about it. I just do it.

So what's the big deal today?

The big deal is that everything in my life is about to change.

You see, I've just asked my longtime sweetie to marry me.

Maggie and I have been together for a long, long time. By together, I mean we have dated exclusively. If we were teenagers, you could say we've been "going steady." We do everything together. We love to dance, eat out, go to movies, or just curl up in front of the TV with a bowl of popcorn. We know each other in the biblical sense as well, and if heaven is half as great as when I'm in her arms, I'll be a happy camper.

What we have *not* done together is occupy the same dwelling. Oh sure, there have been many sleepovers, but these are momentary distractions from the usual, and the next day I am back to my thirty-year routine.

I am reminded of the old joke, "My wife and I had a wonderful relationship. Then we got married."

So why spoil a good thing? I've asked myself that question a bazillion times since I proposed to Maggie at the Sprint Center Arena in front of 19,000 people, dressed as Elvis—but that's another story.

The answer was simple. I didn't want to be alone anymore.

I live on Armour Boulevard in my three-story, brick walk-up. There are five other two-bedroom apartments and a basement apartment all occupied by golden agers that have one thing in common—they are all alone.

We are all close friends; most have been with me over ten years. But at the end of the day, we each retreat to our own inner sanctum, close the door, and spend the night alone.

Since my new vocation seems to require that my body be abused on a regular basis, I've found that nothing heals the body and soul more than coming home to a loving, nurturing woman.

So what was the problem?

I was scared! That's what!

The most frightening thing in the world is the unknown.

What if I was too set in my ways? What if I couldn't change and adapt? What if I spoiled the beautiful relationship we already had? What if—what if?

I guess this is what is known as cold feet.

My consolation is that nothing cures cold feet better than a warm body next to you.

In keeping with my daily routine, I headed to the precinct for squad meeting as I had every morning for almost a year.

The sun was shining, robins scratched in dry leaves looking for the early worm, and at last the long winter seemed to be over. Spring had arrived.

Life was good.

I parked and headed for the locker room. I met Ox, my partner, and we were off to get our daily assignment.

Ox is a twenty-three-year veteran of the force, and at 220 pounds he is the perfect guy to balance my meager 145 pounds. Together we have combined his bulk and police training with my years of life experience and incredible good luck to produce a very respectable arrest record. When not on special assignment, we routinely serve bench warrants and patrol the streets in our ancient black and white Crown Vic.

Today was no exception. My old high school friend and mentor, Captain Short, proudly proclaimed that crime seemed to be taking a holiday and dismissed us all to our regular assignments. We patrolled midtown Kansas City in silence, enjoying the warm sun and each other's company.

Finally Ox broke the silence. "You and Maggie set a date yet?"

Truth be told, since that night at the Sprint Center when I proposed and Maggie accepted, we had both steered away from that subject. I began to wonder if her toes were getting a bit nippy too.

"Actually, no. We're still kind of getting used to the idea."

Thankfully, the topic was interrupted by the car radio. "Car fifty-four, what is your location?"

Ox keyed the mike. "We're at Thirty-seventh and Main."

"Please respond to a disturbance call in the thirty-eight hundred block of Baltimore. A Mrs. Brown will meet you on the street."

"Roger that. On the way. Car fifty-four out."

Like much of midtown Kansas City, this neighborhood consisted of once-elegant two and three-story homes that had been converted from single-family residences to duplexes and triplexes by enterprising landlords.

There is an old saying, "Good fences make good neighbors."

Conversely, when people are living on top of one another, the opportunities for conflict rise dramatically.

As we turned off Thirty-eighth Street onto Baltimore, we saw a middle-aged lady on the sidewalk in front of one of these typical conversions, wildly waving her arms. The woman was obviously distraught. She reminded me of the poor lady in high school who had just spent the day with the kids in the detention room.

"Bet that's Mrs. Brown," I quipped.

"You think?"

Mrs. Brown wasted no time. She was on top of us before we could get the doors closed.

"I've had it! I just can't stand their constant bickering any longer. Somebody's got to do *something*!"

Ox raised his hands. "Whoa. Calm down, Mrs. Brown. Why don't you take a deep breath and start from the beginning."

Before she could reply, a loud crash echoed from the second-floor apartment, along with, "Edgar! You dumb shit! Just look what you've done now!"

Mrs. Brown didn't have to say a word. She just pointed and shook her head. We got the picture.

"How do you want to handle this?" I asked, remembering our last domestic disturbance when I left covered in Chinese takeout.

"Let me take this one," Ox replied. Most folks think twice before getting physical with the Incredible Hulk.

We climbed the stairs to the second-floor unit, and Ox knocked on the door. "Kansas City Police Department. Open up please."

"Get lost! We don't need the cops."

"Sorry, can't do that. We've received a complaint, and we'll have to file a report."

"It's that damn busybody next door, isn't it? Why can't she mind her own business?"

"Open the door please, and let's talk this over."

The door swung open, and we were face to face with the wicked witch of the north. She was in a long, pink robe; her hair was in curlers, and a Marlboro hung from her lower lip.

"Let's get this over with," she growled.

I looked past her and saw a little old guy about my size sweeping peas into a dustpan.

"Okay, what's going on?" Ox asked.

"Ask Einstein over there. It's all his fault."

Ox looked at the crestfallen Edgar.

"Yeah. It's my fault. I didn't mean nothin'. We was just sittin' there talkin' about our anniversary comin' up. Number twenty.

"I asked Wilma where she'd like to go, and she said, 'Somewhere I haven't been in a long time.' All I said was, 'Okay, how about the kitchen?' That's when the fight started."

"So who threw the peas?"

"Who do you think, dimwit? If he don't like eatin' my cookin', I figured he could try wearin' it."

"So you folks do this often?"

"Only when he acts like a dipshit, which is most of the time."

"Anyone ever get hurt?"

"Hell no. Edgar wouldn't lay a finger on me. He'd be afraid to ever sleep again knowing I'd cut his balls off while he was out."

"Actually, I was more concerned about Edgar."

"Oh, so now you're a smartass too!"

I figured I ought to step in at that point.

"Ma'am, what you and your husband do in your own home is nobody's business as long as you don't disturb your neighbors and you don't hurt each other. If you promise to keep a lid on it, I think we can wrap this up."

"Sure, sure, whatever."

"Great. Don't make us come back again because next time we'll have to issue a citation for disturbing the peace."

On our way back to the car, Ox remarked, "How can people live like that? Twenty years of constant bickering. It would drive me crazy. I wonder if they started off that way or it just evolved over time. And if they're so miserable, why stay together?"

This graphic exhibition of matrimonial disharmony wasn't exactly what I needed to help me shake my case of cold feet. In fact, the more I thought about it, the more I questioned what Maggie and I were about to do.

The remainder of the day was uneventful, and I was looking forward to an evening home alone.

Not a good sign.

I was actually relieved when Maggie called and said she had an evening listing appointment.

I had just settled in with a glass of Arbor Mist when the phone rang.

"Walt, it's Mary. I need your help."

Mary Murphy is the resident manager of my Three Trails Hotel and a dear friend.

The hotel and the building I live in are the last vestiges of a rather sizeable rental portfolio that I once had. I sold out lock, stock, and barrel, but no one would buy the hotel. This once-proud structure had evolved over the years into a flophouse for vagrants and druggies. I bought it, kicked everyone out, and remodeled, but it's still a flophouse. Twenty sleeping rooms with bed, dresser, and chair share four hall bathrooms. Plus, there's a small one-bedroom apartment for Mary. Most of my tenants are single, retirees on Social Security, or guys working out of the daily labor pool. They pay by the week—forty bucks a pop.

Mary is a young, robust seventy-six and weighs in at about 200 pounds. She rules the hotel with an iron hand, and her weapon of choice is a thirty-six-inch, white ash Hillrich and Bradsby baseball bat. No one wins an argument with Mary.

"What's up, Mary? How can I help?"

"I've got a vacancy, so I put up my 'for rent' sign. And I've got a guy here who wants to rent a room. I know I don't usually bother you with this kind of stuff, but this is just too weird."

"Weird? How so?"

"Long story. Can you come over? You'll want to see this for yourself."

"Okay, on my way."

So much for a quiet evening alone.

I drove the eight blocks to Linwood Avenue, and as I pulled to the curb I saw a mid-fifties guy in a white shirt and tie sitting on the porch swing. I was beginning to get the picture. I would be willing to bet there isn't another tie amongst all of the other nineteen tenants in the building.

Incredibly, the first thing I noticed when the guy rose to greet me was the absence of ear and nose hair. The other occupants of the hotel seem to view this as a badge of honor.

At that moment, Mary emerged from her apartment decked out in her best floral muumuu, which I knew from past experience was only worn on special occasions.

"Hey, Mr. Walt. This is Lawrence Wingate. He wants to rent number twenty. I thought you might want to visit with him." She gave me a wink.

"Pleased to meet you, Mr. Williams," Wingate said as he extended his hand.

"Likewise, Mr. Wingate."

I noticed his hands were as smooth as a baby's butt. This guy didn't work out of the labor pool.

"If you have an application, I'd like to be considered for your vacant unit."

Mary gave me a big grin. Our usual method of tenant selection for the hotel was to hold a mirror up to the guy's mouth. If he had enough breath to fog it, wasn't a fleeing felon, and had the first week's rent, he was in.

"Uh, we're not that formal here, Mr. Wingate. Not to be nosey, but you don't exactly fit the profile of our usual tenant."

"No, probably not. I would venture a guess that not many men have experienced what I have over the last six months."

Now my curiosity was aroused.

"It certainly isn't a requirement for acceptance into the hotel, but if you'd care to elaborate, I'm all ears."

"You bet I would. In fact, one of the driving forces in my life right now is to warn any man who will listen of the evils of the feminine mind."

Oh great! This was just what I needed.

"Six months ago, at the age of fifty-five, I suffered a heart attack and had to undergo a quadruple bypass surgery."

"Looks like you made it through okay."

"My body is fine; everything else in my life, not so much. You see, my loving wife, Florence, of twenty-two years cleaned me out and left me penniless."

"Say what?"

"I'm sure you're aware that the risks involved in that type of invasive surgery are enormous. Some just don't make it off the table, or if they do, they are incapacitated for long periods of time. As part of getting my affairs in order, I signed my power-of-attorney over to my wife before they cracked me open."

"Sounds like the right thing to do."

"I thought so too, until I came out of recovery and discovered that my sweet wife had used the power-of-attorney to sell our house and clean out our bank accounts. Florence had obviously been planning this for some time. She had a buyer ready to close before the ink dried. Friends tell me she is somewhere in Hawaii living the good life."

"Wow!" was all I could muster. Wingate's story hit me between the eyes like a two-by-four.

"So I'm basically penniless and starting from scratch. Fortunately, I still have my job. That's about the only thing she couldn't take away from me."

"What type of work do you do?"

"Computer geek. I'm in charge of the computer system for a large insurance company. Too bad there's no insurance for marital fraud. So how about that room? It's all I can afford right now."

"Of course you can have the room. Actually, I'm embarrassed to rent it to you. It's not exactly Motel Six, but we do keep the lights on for you."

"Not a problem. I'll have to crawl for a while before I can walk again."

"Mary will get you checked in, won't you, Mary?"

"You bet I will. I'll take real good care of Mr. Wingate."

I'd never heard Mary call anyone "mister" but me.

I had been so engrossed in Wingate's tale of woe that I hadn't noticed three of our elderly tenants had congregated on the other end of the porch.

As I mentioned, twenty tenants share four common toilets, and given the complex bowel functions of the aged, bathroom banter is often the topic of conversation.

I couldn't help but hear their conversation and hoped that Mr. Wingate was too busy with Mary to pay attention. It wasn't pretty.

Seventy-year-old Mr. Feeny from number fourteen spoke first. "I have this problem. I wake up every morning at seven, and it takes me twenty minutes to pee."

Eighty-two-year-old Mr. Barnes from number sixteen chimed in, "My case is worse. I get up at eight and sit there and grunt and groan for half an hour before I finally have a bowel movement."

But Mr. Cobb from number twelve topped them all. "At seven, I pee like a horse, and at eight I crap like a cow."

"So what's your problem?" asked the others.

"I don't wake up until nine!"

As I drove back to my building, I wasn't sure which troubled me most, Mr. Cobb's incontinence or Mr. Wingate's marital meltdown.

After reflecting on both, I concluded that since I was not quite ready for Depends and I was about to tie the knot, it was the latter.

Actually, it may have been the combination of both because at that moment the idea of marriage scared me shitless!

$$\text{⚖}$$

The next day Ox and I were on our usual rounds when the radio crackled, "Car fifty-four, if you're in the vicinity of Thirty-eighth and Baltimore, please respond to another disturbance call."

"Roger that. Car fifty-four out."

"Sounds like Edgar and Wilma are at it again."

An irate Mrs. Brown met us at the curb. "I thought you two were going to take care of this," she bellowed.

"Now calm down. What's going on?"

"They're at it already. I can't even have my morning coffee in peace without listening to their screaming."

We heard another loud crash and, "Dust this, you peckerhead!"

Oh boy!

Once again we climbed the stairs. We didn't even have time to knock. By the time we reached the second floor, poor Edgar was standing in the open door, his face contorted in fear.

"Get me out of here! I just can't do this anymore."

We peered into the living room and saw a wild-eyed Wilma standing over the remnants of a small portable TV.

"Why does that little shit have to provoke me all the time? It's all his fault!"

We looked at Edgar.

"I didn't mean nothin'. We had just sat down with our coffee, and I picked up the remote. She asked me, 'What's on TV?' All I said was, 'Dust,' and that's when the fight started."

"That's it," Ox said. "You two need some help. Get your coats. We're going to the station."

Thankfully, Ox called for backup, and we took them to the station in separate cars. There was no way we were going to listen to World War III all the way downtown.

We made the trip in silence, but I was actually hoping for a distraction from the frightening scenario that was playing in my mind.

My thoughts of Maggie are always pleasant. She's a tender, loving woman whose sweet smile warms my heart.

But at that moment, I was terrified by the specter of a snarling Maggie with curlers in her hair and a cigarette dangling from her lip.

By the time we reached the station, my rational self had prevailed. *After all*, I told myself, *Maggie doesn't even smoke.*

Maggie is still an active real estate agent, which means she has no set schedule. She works when the business is there. Most of the time we are able to juggle things so that we can be together at least part of each day, but her schedule had been so hectic that it had been three days since we had time together.

I was really missing her.

She called and said her six o'clock had canceled, so she was free for the evening. We decided to order in and watch some TV.

Maggie arrived about the same time as the pizza guy. We popped open a bottle of Arbor Mist Peach Chardonnay and settled in for a romantic evening together.

One of the things that has made our relationship work is our honesty with one another. We have each been able to share our feelings and concerns without the other one getting bent out of shape. Tonight, something felt different.

She caught me up on her latest real estate transactions, and I mumbled something stupid about my day. I didn't really want to get into my brush with marital discord.

I noticed that we both steered the conversation away from our upcoming nuptials, which was okay with me.

I grabbed the remote and started flipping through channels and landed on a Julia Roberts marathon.

"Oh, I love Julia Roberts," she purred. "Can we watch that?"

"Why not?"

I soon found out why not.

Which Julia Roberts's flick did we get?

You guessed it—*Runaway Bride*.

CHAPTER TWO

The next morning at squad meeting, Captain Short introduced Captain Michael Barnes from the northeast division.

"Gentlemen, Captain Barnes is here to bring us up to date on recent gang activity in the northeast precinct and how it may impact our area. I'm sure you all remember the Niners. Give him a listen."

I remembered the Niners all right. Ox and I were doing perimeter backup when the tactical squad raided the gang's drug distribution center. The leader of the Niners, Duane, or Lil D, slipped through the net and headed our direction. We followed him to an abandoned board-up. The ensuing confrontation was my first gunfight and introduction to K.C.'s canine unit.

In the end, a lucky shot from my .22 caliber peashooter struck Lil D's left nut and left him impotent, indignant, and outraged. It also brought the gang's activities to a halt.

"We thought that with Lil D out of the picture, the Niners would not regroup," Captain Barnes began. "Unfortunately, that has not been the case. Lil D's older brother, Jerome, has come to Kansas City from Detroit, where he led a similar gang, and he's brought some muscle with him.

"His goal seems to be to revive the Niners and seek retribution for the suffering of his little brother."

Oh great. That's just what I wanted to hear.

"The Niners' former territory had been north and east of your midtown area, but two factors have changed all that. Number one, the latest urban renewal project has cut a big chunk out of their area of influence, and two, they know that the officer responsible for Lil D's incarceration and humiliation works in midtown." He looked directly at me.

I hope he's not one of those eye-for-an-eye kind of guys, I thought, and my hand involuntarily assumed a protective position over Mr. Winkie and the boys.

"He's one mean son of a bitch," the captain continued. "The new Niners are tough. To be accepted, a new member must pass two tests; the first is to successfully pull off an armed robbery, and the second is to abduct a white woman for—well, you can imagine what for.

"Two convenience stores on the east side have already been hit, and a young woman was abducted from a mall parking lot. She was found alive in a vacant lot, but she had been beaten and gang-raped. I'm afraid this is just the beginning.

"We have no leads as to the whereabouts of Jerome and the gang, and street people, including our usual snitches, won't talk to us. Can't say I blame them."

"Thank you for the update, Captain. We obviously can't be everywhere," Captain Short continued, "but we are going to increase our physical presence on the street. All available units will patrol commercial areas with malls and convenience stores. I'm sure I don't have to remind any of you of the potential pitfalls of racial profiling, but the Niners are a black gang, so be vigilant."

The captain dismissed us, and we picked up our assignments and headed to the black and white.

Neither of us spoke for a while, and finally I had to ask.

"Ox, you've been at this for over twenty years, and you've had hundreds of collars. Have any of them ever tried to get even?"

"No, not with me. Most crooks know that getting caught is just part of the game. We're just doing our job, and they don't take it personal. But once in a while, one comes along. I've known a few cops, a prosecutor, and a judge who were targets for revenge. Walt, you've got to be on your toes."

Beginner's luck, I guess.

I returned home that evening with the thoughts of a vengeful gangbanger festering in my mind.

How was I supposed to deal with it?

I couldn't just dismiss it—the threat was real—but I also couldn't allow it to consume my every waking moment.

I looked around my empty apartment, and I felt frightened and very alone.

Then the phone rang.

"Hi, Walt. It's Maggie."

Maggie! What was I supposed to do about her? How could I even think about being with her when some crazy black dude was looking for an opportunity to whack me?

"Maggie, we need to talk." I told her the whole story.

"Walt, are you ready to quit the department?"

Her question caught me off guard. I hadn't really followed my fears to this conclusion.

"Well, uh . . ." I stammered. "Not really."

"Then I only have one thing to say to you. If you're bound and determined to be Clark Kent, then I'm going to be Lois Lane. It's a package deal."

"But—"

"No buts. I love you, and we're in this together—for better or for worse."

I think I've heard that line before.

"Okay, now that we've got that over with, let me tell you why I called. You know I've been working with Mr. Finch. He's been hired by the Nelson Art Gallery, and we finally found the right home for him and his family. He gave me two complimentary tickets to the Ancient Egypt exhibit at the gallery. We're both off tomorrow. How about it?"

How could I refuse?

As I hung up the phone, I couldn't help but smile as I thought of Maggie and me as Clark Kent and Lois Lane. That was the "for better" part.

Then I thought of Jerome and the Niners and the women who had been abducted and raped. That was certainly the "for worse" part.

At that moment, I couldn't think of anything worse than putting Maggie in harm's way.

I picked Maggie up at nine thirty, and we headed to the art gallery.

Human beings are strange creatures.

The Nelson Art Gallery is one of the premier tourist attractions in the city.

I have lived in the Kansas City area all my life, and this would be just the second time my shadow had darkened its doors.

People come from all over the world to enjoy the fabulous works of art housed there.

I too have traveled hundreds of miles to distant locations and visited galleries and museums of lesser quality, so why hadn't I enjoyed the beauty right in my own backyard?

I believe it's one of the foibles of human nature; we often take the things closest to us for granted. We just assume they'll always be there.

I think that also applies to the people around us, and that's what was going through my mind as we drove to the gallery.

I thought of the special lady sitting next to me who was willing to stick by me, for better or for worse, and it occurred to me that I was such a dumbass for listening to my cold feet.

We decided to make a day of it. We would roam the halls and enjoy the exhibits until noon and then enjoy lunch in the beautiful Rozzelle Court Restaurant.

We found the Egyptian exhibit in Gallery L11 of the Bloch Building and were enthralled by the grandeur of the Great Pyramid and the Sphinx. The beauty and intricacy of the artwork and carvings found in the tombs of kings left us breathless.

While my usual dining preference was the comfort food served at Mel's Diner on Broadway, it was not Maggie's favorite place to eat.

We both knew, however, that much in life is a compromise. Maggie would go to Mel's with me, and I, in turn, would take her to one of the classier joints.

Neither of us were disappointed by the fare at the Rozzelle Restaurant. We wolfed down spaghetti and meatballs served with green beans almandine with roasted red peppers, buttered noodles, and a fresh baked roll. We topped it off with black coffee and huge slices of Nelson's key lime pie.

Life was good!

Stuffed to the gills, we made our way to the Nelson-Atkins building and wandered by Gallery 222 just as a guest lecture was about to begin.

"I'm so full I can hardly waddle," Maggie proclaimed. "How about we just go in, sit, and listen while our lunch settles?"

Looking back, it makes one wonder what forces are at play when such seemingly insignificant decisions change the course of our lives. Is it fate, serendipity, blind luck, or something else?

The lecture was titled, "The History and Culture of the Ancient Hawaiians."

We took our seats along with maybe a dozen others and were greeted by an elderly, gray-haired gentleman who identified himself as Raymond Kalakoa. He said we could call him Uncle Ray.

The exhibit was part of a recently discovered burial site found in a cave opening in a sheer rock cliff inside a dormant volcano. The items on display were new to the world, but the story Uncle Ray shared with us had been passed from generation to generation for centuries.

His story, visually augmented with slides from the beautiful islands of the Hawaiian chain, told of the voyages of the early Polynesians across three thousand miles of open ocean, over three hundred years before the birth of Christ. He told of the colonization of the islands and the social structure of the early Hawaiians with their *alii*, or chiefs, and their *kahuna*, or priests.

Each phase of their early history was brought to life by the artifacts that were on display. We could visualize the pounding of the taro plant into poi with the stone mallet and bowl. The magnificent feathered capes, headgear, and *kahili* of the chiefs bore testimony of their royalty, and the war clubs of *koa* inset with razor sharp shark's teeth were a grim reminder that men throughout the centuries have fought one another to the death.

We sat spellbound as Uncle Ray shared the history of his early ancestors. It was more than just an old man telling a story; it was almost as if he were a vessel through which the chiefs and priests from generations past were speaking.

He seemed to be almost in a trance as he spoke, but suddenly his countenance changed, and he looked around the room and stared into the eyes of each listener, one by one.

Finally, his piercing gaze fell on Maggie, and as he stared into her eyes, we heard the words *akua* and *mana*.

His gaze shifted to me, back to Maggie, and then to me again.

It felt as if he had used my eyes to gain entry into my soul. It was a sensation I had never felt before or since.

My eyes were locked with his, and he muttered, "*Kane, kokua.*"

Just as abruptly as it had come, his countenance reverted back to good old Uncle Ray. He thanked everyone for their attendance and hoped they enjoyed the presentation. Then he pointed to Maggie and me.

"You stay!"

After everyone else had departed, he knelt down in front of us.

"My homeland calls to you. It is not yours to understand now, but the day will come. You have been chosen."

We both sat there dumbfounded.

He turned to Maggie. "You are to be called Hualani." Then he turned to me. "And you are Kamamalu."

He reached into a pouch he carried around his waist and removed a small object carved from black obsidian. It was a lizard.

"Take *mo'o'ala*. He is your *aumakua*. He will guide you."

He pressed the tiny lizard into the palm of my hand.

"You go now, but remember my words, and listen in your hearts for the call of the *aina*."

He rose and left us alone.

We sat there speechless, trying to make sense of what had just transpired. I could have almost believed it was a dream were it not for the obsidian lizard I clutched in my hand.

Maggie spoke first. "Walt, what just happened?"

"I was hoping you could tell me."

"Please don't laugh when I tell you this. It sounds so stupid now."

"Tell me what?"

"You know I've never been to any of the Hawaiian Islands."

"Right."

"While Uncle Ray was showing the slides, I had the distinct feeling I had been there before. It was like when I returned to my childhood home for the first time after many years. Everything had changed, but there was an instinctual recognition of places and events. I can't describe it any other way."

"Are you as creeped out as I am?"

"Probably more!"

On the way home we did our best to recall every word that Uncle Ray had spoken to us and wrote it all down as best we could.

We were on Main Street, just a few minutes from Maggie's apartment on the Plaza, when she exclaimed, "Oh, rats! I almost forgot. I'm totally out of milk. Can we pull into a 7-Eleven? I'll just be a minute."

I pulled into the first convenience store I could find and noticed that the gas gauge was leaning toward empty.

"I'll gas up while you're shopping."

Maggie headed into the store, and I started pumping. I set the nozzle on automatic and leaned back against the side of the car, my mind still pondering our strange encounter with Uncle Ray.

Suddenly, gas spewed from the tank and drenched my trousers. The automatic shut-off had failed to engage. By the time I manually shut down the pump, I was dripping with high octane.

"Well, crap! I'm going to need a shower just to get home." I headed for the men's room on the side of the building.

I thought I heard shouting from inside the store, but the walls were thick, and the water was running. I soaped up and de-gassed as best I could.

I exited the men's room just in time to see a black Chevy minivan burn rubber out of the parking lot.

People began pouring out of the store, some crying, some screaming.

I grabbed a young kid by the arm. "What in the world's going on?"

"Robbery! And they took her!"

"Took who?"

"Some lady with red hair."

My heart leaped into my throat.

"Maggie!"

I ran into the store and found the manager, who had just called 911.

I flashed my badge. "Quick! Tell me what happened!"

"A black man with a gun came to the counter and demanded money. I gave him all that was in the register. A red-haired woman had just come to the counter with a gallon of milk. He took the money, grabbed the woman, and ran out of the store."

My heart sank.

"What did he look like?"

"He was a black dude."

"Yes, you said that. What else? Surely you can do better than that."

"He was tall. Oh yeah, he held the gun in his right hand, and I saw two sixes tattooed on his wrist."

No, not sixes; they were nines, and they were badges of honor earned for two previous abductions.

I slumped to the floor and leaned against the counter. I felt like all the life had just been sucked out of me.

I was still there when the first officer arrived on the scene. It was my friend and first recruit into the C.R.A.P. program.

"Vince, they've got Maggie!"

CHAPTER THREE

As soon as Vince reported that Maggie was the abductee, a dozen police cruisers converged on the convenience store. Even the captain came and personally took charge of the investigation.

I was a total wreck.

"Walt, go home," the captain ordered.

"But—"

"You're in no shape to help us right now. Let us do our job. I'll have Vince call you the minute we know anything. Now go!"

I stumbled into my car and headed toward Armour Boulevard.

As I thought of Maggie in the hands of those bastards, I was overcome with grief, and another wave of uncontrollable sobbing wracked my body. I pulled to the side of the street and waited until the tears subsided.

When the wave had passed, I just sat there. I was an emotional wreck, and I could think of nothing but the void in my life without Maggie.

Eventually I became aware of an uncomfortable sensation. Something was poking me in the area of my groin.

I fished around in my pocket and discovered the cause of my discomfort, a tiny black lizard.

I clutched the amulet in my hand and reflected upon the events of the day. In just a few short hours, my life had transformed from a state of bliss and contentment to one of grief and regret.

As I gazed at the lizard, I recalled Uncle Ray's words, "Take *mo'o'ala*. He is your *aumakua*. He will guide you."

I almost laughed as I looked again at the tiny bauble in my hand.

"Superstitious old fool," I muttered bitterly.

But then I also remembered the sensation I felt as Uncle Ray's eyes peered into the depths of my soul. I clutched the amulet in my hand and pressed it against my chest.

"I could use some help right now."

A feeling of calm spread through my body, and my mind, which had been clouded with grief and self-pity, suddenly cleared. It was almost like the sun breaking through the gloom after a summer storm.

A verse from the old 1972 Johnny Nash song came to mind:

> I can see clearly now, the rain has gone.
> I can see all the obstacles in my way.

I knew what I had to do.

I pulled to the curb in front of my building, and as I'd hoped, my old friend Willie Duncan was sitting on the porch steps.

Willie lives in the basement apartment and takes care of the maintenance of my two buildings. I met Willie years ago when he was a street hustler. We hit it off, and he has been with me ever since. While Willie has given up his life of petty larceny, he has maintained his relationship with his old friends on the seamier side of town. As a trusted friend from the old days, Willie is sometimes privy to information known only to the street people.

Riding on Willie's shirttail, I have developed a you-scratch-my-back-and-I'll-scratch-yours relationship with various hookers and con men. More than once, these relationships have helped us bring down some really bad dudes, and more than once Willie and his cohorts have saved my sorry ass.

As I approached, I was greeted by Willie's favorite salutation, "Hey, Mr. Walt. How's it hanging?"

"It's hanging pretty low right now. Willie, I need your help. They've got Maggie."

"Who's got Maggie?"

"The Niners."

"Oh, Mr. Walt. Dat's bad news. Dem guys is just plain crazy."

I told Willie about the gang's initiation rites and about Maggie's abduction. "So far, no one's been able to put a finger on Jerome, the head guy. I have to talk to him."

"From what I hear, Jerome don't talk to nobody. He jus' hurts people."

"Surely someone on the street knows how to get in touch with Jerome. How about Louie the Lip?"

"No, sir! Louie and guys like me don't want nothin' to do wit dem crazy dudes."

"I'm not saying he runs with them, but I'd bet he knows where they hang out. Please, will you talk to him?"

Reluctantly, Willie agreed, and we headed for Louie's corner on Independence Avenue.

While Louie and I weren't exactly on a first-name basis, he and Willie had helped subdue a mob hit man who had killed Doris, who was a hooker and mutual friend.

Louie climbed into the car and gave me a nod.

"Hey, bro."

For the third time that day, I told the story of Maggie's abduction.

Louie sat in silence. Finally he said, "I like you, man. But you dealing with some serious shit here. Since Jerome come to town, he got two things on his mind: hurtin' white folks and findin' de guy what shot his brudda. If Jerome find out I even talkin' to you, I won't last a day."

"I would think that Jerome would think kindly about the guy who brought his brother's shooter to him. What do you think?"

"Well sho. But what guy is gonna be stupid enough to walk up to Jerome and admit he shot his brother?"

"I would."

"Shit, man! You de dude that shot Lil D?"

"Yep, and I want to make a deal: me for Maggie. Can you get in touch with him?"

"If Jerome finds out you de guy, you a dead man for sure. It's crazy, man."

I turned to Willie. "If there was any way you could have saved Doris, what would you have done?"

Willie looked at me and turned to Louie. "Make de call."

I knew he would understand.

"Wait here," Louie ordered. A few minutes later he returned with a slip of paper. "Here's a number where you can contact Jerome. I didn't say nothin' except you had information on who shot his brudda. Good luck, man. You gonna need it."

I thanked him, and I headed back to the apartment to drop Willie off.

"Okay, Mr. Walt. What we gonna do?"

"*We* aren't going to do anything. You're done. You're out of it. From here on, it's all me."

"But you gonna call Ox and Vince, right?"

"Nope. If Jerome finds out I brought the cops, Maggie won't have a chance."

"But what you gonna do?"

"What I'm going to do is get Maggie out of there, and what you're going to do is go home and take care of things until I get back."

"Walt, you my bes' friend. I couldn't do nothin' to help Doris. Please let me help you."

A plan began to form in my mind.

"Okay, you can help, but you have to do *exactly* what I tell you, no questions asked."

"I promise."

I dropped Willie at the apartment and drove to an underground garage on Broadway. I parked, pulled out my cell phone, and dialed the number.

"Yeah."

"I want to talk to Jerome."

"Who's dis?"

"Someone with information."

"Jerome don' talk to nobody less he knows 'em. Get lost."

"Don't you think Jerome would like to talk to the guy who shot his brother?"

Silence.

"Dis Jerome. Who de hell is this?"

"I'm the guy who shot the left nut off your pansy-ass brother."

"Den you a dead man."

"Not unless you can find me, and I promise that's not going to happen unless I want it to."

"Why you callin'?"

"Because I have something you want, and you have something I want."

"What I got that you want?"

"The red-haired woman who was taken from the 7-Eleven today."

"She one fine bitch. We gonna have fun with her tonight."

"If you touch her, I promise you'll never have your revenge on the guy who put your punk brother in prison to rot."

"What you got in mind?"

"Me for the redhead, even exchange."

"You think I'm stupid. You a damn cop."

"No cops, I promise."

"Here's de deal. You come alone to de warehouse on—"

"No, here's the deal. There's a Starbucks on the corner of Armour and Broadway. We'll meet there. You bring the redhead and anybody else you want. I'll be there with a friend. He's not a cop. I promise, no cops. I'll be unarmed, and I won't be wearing a wire. You can check me out before the exchange. When you're satisfied, my friend takes the redhead and leaves, and when they're gone, I'm all yours."

"Listen, punk, you don't make de rules."

"I do this time. It's my way or the highway. Oh, and I'll be sure to get the word on the street that you're as big a coward as your chicken-shit brother."

I could almost feel the heat through the phone.

"Eight o'clock, and if anything goes wrong, the bitch is dead."

I picked Willie up at seven thirty, and we headed toward Broadway.

"Now remember what I told you. They're going to check me for wires and guns. When they're satisfied, they will produce Maggie for the exchange. As soon as she is in your hands, get her out of there as fast as you can. If she's been hurt, take her to the hospital; if not, take her straight to the precinct. She's going to protest and not want to leave me there, but I'm counting on you to get her out of harm's way. No heroics. Can you do that for me?"

"Sho, but what you gonna do?"

"Don't worry. I have a plan."

Actually, I didn't. My only goal was to get Maggie back. I didn't have a clue what I would do after that.

I found a parking spot on Broadway about a block from Starbucks. I handed Willie the keys, and we embraced.

"Take care of my girl."

At eight fifteen, no one had showed. I wasn't surprised. Jerome was no dummy. I'm sure he had been watching the coffee shop for hours before our appointed time, and he was still watching to be sure we weren't tailed.

At eight thirty we saw a black guy heading our direction. "Follow me," he ordered.

"I'm not going anywhere. That wasn't the deal. Pat me down, check me out any way you want, but we're doing it right here."

The guy glanced over his shoulder and apparently got the go-ahead. As unobtrusively as possible, he patted and poked until he was satisfied and gave another nod over his shoulder.

A tall black man emerged from the parking lot at the rear of the coffee shop. It was Jerome, and he had Maggie.

Our eyes met, and I saw her fear when she realized what was about to transpire.

She opened her mouth to speak, but I shook my head. She fell silent.

I looked Jerome in the eye. His face was contorted into a malevolent grin. I could only imagine the pleasure he had felt as he conjured ways to exact his revenge.

"You ready to do this?"

"Let's do it, man. I got some big plans for you."

He pushed Maggie in my direction. I took her hand and whisked her back and into Willie's waiting arms. I whispered, "I love you," in her ear and turned to Willie. "Go! Now!"

Maggie resisted, as I knew she would, but Willie was a man of his word and pushed her forcefully into the waiting car. I saw the taillights disappear around the corner and turned to Jerome. "I'm all yours."

I was led to the parking lot at the rear of the coffee shop and shoved into the same Chevy van that had taken Maggie.

I noted that they didn't bother to blindfold me as we traveled the streets of Kansas City to their gang hangout. I took that as a bad omen; they knew I would never be leaving.

We drove in circles for about an hour. I figured they were checking for tails.

Finally satisfied, they headed for St. John Avenue, and we pulled into the driveway of an old brick building that had once housed a Wonder Bread Thrift Store. The big metal door rolled up, and we parked next to the old loading dock.

I was led through a set of swinging doors into a large, open room. I wasn't prepared for the spectacle that met my eyes.

An empty chair sat at one end of the room, and at least thirty more chairs were set in a semi-circle, each one occupied by a member of the gang.

This had obviously been billed as a special event, and I was the main attraction.

I think at that moment I had a pretty good idea how the Christians might have felt as they were led into the arena of the Colosseum. If I had a choice, I probably would have chosen the lions over Jerome. At least the lions would get it over with quickly. I didn't think that's what Jerome had in mind.

I was led to the empty chair and told to sit.

Jerome strode to the center of the room. A hush fell as the assembled gang members waited anxiously for their leader to speak.

"Dis is a great day. Your leader, my brother, has been disrespected by dis man, and dis is de day we exacts our revenge." He turned and walked up to me. "Are you de man that shot Lil D?"

I looked up at the tall black man silhouetted under the big glass skylight in the roof of the building.

"Yes, I am."

"Are you sorry you shot my brother?"

"No, sir, I am not."

A collective gasp arose from the gang members.

I had remembered seeing newsreel footage of American soldiers who had been captured by Middle East terrorists and had marveled at the outward calm they seemed to possess. I think that calm comes from knowing that your fate is no longer under your control and the last thing you possess that is yours alone is your dignity.

"Your brother was a filthy scumbag who sold drugs to children and terrorized this city. He got what he deserved, and I would gladly do it again."

On reflection, that probably wasn't the smartest thing I could have said.

Jerome hit me squarely across the face with the back of his hand and sent me sprawling on the concrete floor. "Now it is time to pay. You shot my brother and disgraced him. You took away his manhood. An eye for an eye. Remove his pants."

I was jerked unceremoniously to my feet, and one guy held my arms while another one unbuckled my belt and dropped my pants around my ankles.

So much for dignity.

"Now you will know the suffering of my brother."

He drew a pistol from his belt, and the men holding me quickly backed away.

I bit my lip and looked down at Mr. Winkie for what I assumed would be the last time. We had had some great times together. I swear I think he was pouting.

I heard the *click* as Jerome pulled back the hammer of the pistol. I closed my eyes and waited.

Instead of the pistol report I had expected, I heard a loud crash, and glass rained down on us from the shattered skylight overhead. The crash was followed by men descending on ropes with weapons drawn. Simultaneously, the outer doors burst open, and a flood of officers in flak jackets and helmets stormed the room.

The Niners were caught unaware. It was over as quickly as it had begun.

I couldn't move. I just stood there like a dumbass while my fellow officers cuffed the last of the gang.

Then I heard a familiar voice. "Hey, partner, you might want to pull your pants up."

I bent over to grab my trousers and came face to face with Mr. Winkie. It was probably that I was still in shock, just a figment of my imagination. I didn't really believe he could actually smile.

"Ox, how—?"

"Captain Short, of course. He's no fool. He told you to go home knowing full well that you'd do something stupid like this. He had Vince tailing you from the moment you left the 7-Eleven."

"So you guys knew all along?"

"Yep."

"And you used me as bait to lead you the Niners?"

"Yep."

"You assholes! You damn near got me shot."

"Hmm, so that's the gratitude we get for saving your sorry ass? Oh, by the way, I think there's someone outside who wants to see you."

I walked into the cool night air of the parking lot and saw Maggie standing with Vince and Willie. She ran into my arms and just held me for the longest time. Finally, she spoke.

"Vince told me you didn't know about the police backup."

I didn't answer.

"So you concocted this whole exchange thing and didn't have a clue how it was going to end?"

I didn't know what to say.

"So you were willing to give your life to save mine?"

"My life wouldn't have been worth much without you."

"Nor mine without you."

"Isn't that what love is all about?"

CHAPTER FOUR

Maggie stayed the night at my apartment.

Both of us had believed that the love of our life had been taken from us forever, and we spent the night in each other's arms, thanking the Big Guy for giving us another chance.

We awoke as dawn's first rays peeked through the bedroom curtains.

"Maggie, I have a confession to make."

"What have you done now?"

"I want to be with you more than anything in this world, but I have to tell you, since that night at the Sprint Center, I've been scared to death."

"So then it's not just me?"

"You too?"

"Walt, we're sixty-seven years old. I've always lived alone, and so have you. We're set in our ways. This is going to be quite a new trick for a couple of old dogs to learn."

"I didn't want to say anything and make you think that I don't love you. You're the best thing in my life."

"I felt the same. I guess if we had been honest with each other, we could have saved ourselves a lot of grief."

"Then let's agree right here and now that we will always be honest and not hide our feelings."

"It's a deal."

I soon discovered why guys don't make deals like that.

We suddenly found ourselves famished and headed to the kitchen for breakfast.

I like to keep life simple, especially early in the morning. I put on a pot of coffee, get the newspaper, and read it over a bowl of Wheaties. When I'm through, I have a little wire rack thingy that holds my cup, spoon, and bowl after they're washed, and they are there waiting for me the next morning.

I put the coffee on and pulled the Wheaties out of the cupboard.

Maggie looked at the Wheaties with disdain. "I guess you don't have any granola. You know, something with some fiber?"

"Fiber? Uh, no. Probably not, but I'll look into it."

"Then I guess Wheaties it is."

I took the bowl out of the wire thingy and looked in the cabinet for another bowl. I actually had four place settings of just dishes and cups, but up till now, one bowl had been adequate.

"You only have one bowl?"

"Uh, looks that way. Oh, wait. Here's an empty Cool Whip container. I can eat out of that."

Problem solved, but I made a mental note to get another bowl and something with "fiber," whatever that is.

I went for the paper while Maggie poured the coffee and Wheaties.

Teamwork! I love it!

It turned out that my little two-seat dinette table was just perfect for one guy and his paper. Double that, and encroachment became an issue.

I was just spreading out when Maggie approached with her coffee and cereal.

"Where am I supposed to eat?"

I surveyed the familiar terrain and immediately discovered the problem.

"Dopey me. Sorry about that."

I folded my paper and set it aside. Maybe later.

Breakfast concluded without further incident, and we headed to the bathroom.

My building was constructed in the 1930s. The apartments are adequate but certainly not spacious by today's standards. I've seen walk-in closets bigger than my bedroom. My unit is a two bedroom with a Jack-and-Jill bath connecting the two. It has one tiny, little sink.

Maggie had stocked a few provisions in the medicine cabinet for our occasional sleepovers.

We each grabbed our toothbrush and started lathering up.

As luck would have it, we both leaned toward the bowl to spit at the same time.

"Ohmp, solly. You 'pit."

"No, you 'pit."

"Radies fust."

Split!

Splat!

It's all a matter of timing.

Dental hygiene had just concluded when Maggie whispered in my ear.

"I think I may need some time alone."

"Have I done something wrong?"

You know, the old guilt thing.

"No, silly. I just need some bathroom time."

"Oh, got it." I made a hasty exit.

Again, modern bathrooms have the commode in a tiny little room with a door, just off the main bath area. My throne is prominently displayed as the main attraction.

It doesn't matter how intimate a couple may have been, there are just some things you don't share. This is one of them.

With all the emphasis on togetherness today, I still can't recall any pundit declaring, "The family that poops together stays together." In fact, it's probably quite the opposite.

I figured this might be a good time to read my paper, and I hoped I would have time to at least get through the sports page. I needn't have worried.

I finished the sports page, expecting Maggie to emerge from the loo at any time. When she didn't appear, I started the front section, then the business section, and finally the comics.

Having finished breakfast and my paper, I too began to get signals from Mother Nature.

"You okay in there?"

"Sure. Be right out." But she wasn't.

My approach to bathroom time is much like my approach to shopping—get in and get it done. If I go to buy socks, I buy socks, and I'm out of there. Maggie, on the other hand, will go into a store for nylons and spend twenty minutes looking at slacks before she hits the stocking aisle.

I couldn't help but wonder what was taking so long. It must just be one of those guy/gal things.

Fortunately, she relinquished the throne just in time. Any further delay would have resulted in me shopping for some new socks—and shorts too.

It was a beautiful spring morning, and we decided to take a walk. As we strolled down Armour Boulevard, I decided to bring up the topic we had both avoided.

"You know, we've never actually set a date yet."

"Yeah, I know."

"Have you thought about what kind of wedding you would like to have?"

I know I had thought about it, and as hard as I tried, I couldn't seem to muster any enthusiasm for the actual event. The only thing that was important to me was to be with Maggie. I would do whatever was necessary to make that happen.

But I'm not stupid. I'm well aware that weddings are all about the bride. It's her special day, and I wanted it to be special for Maggie.

"I've thought about it, but I don't know what I want. It doesn't seem quite appropriate for a sixty-seven-year-old woman to walk down an aisle in a wedding gown. I don't even know if I want a church wedding. I've thought about the rose garden at Loose Park, but I just don't know."

"So are you thinking something big or a small intimate thing with just close friends?"

"I don't want anything big. You know, just the people closest to us."

"Well, we both worked at City Wide Realty. We'd probably want our friends there to attend. Plus some of our realtor friends from other offices. Oh, and our loan guy and our termite guy and the inspector."

"And what about your fellow officers from the precinct? How many would that be?

"Probably thirty."

"Then there's Willie and his friends and Mary and the professor and…"

So much for a small wedding.

We thoroughly enjoyed our early morning walk, but we were no closer to being hitched than the night I proposed.

At least now we were talking about it.

CHAPTER FIVE

With Jerome and the Niners out of commission, activity at the precinct was scaled back to the usual routine.

Unfortunately, part of the usual routine was to give a ration of shit to the old geezer who had, once again, set himself up as the comic relief of the squad room.

My fellow officers were not about to let me forget that I was standing in a warehouse surrounded by black gangbangers with my trousers down around my ankles and Mr. Winkie and the boys exposed to the world when the whole squad burst in for the rescue.

I had heard comments like, "If you guys were comparing 'equipment,' I'm afraid you came out on the 'short' end."

Today, when I walked into the squad room, they were ready for me.

Someone hit play on the boombox, and the words of the cult hit introduced on *American Idol* filled the room:

> Pants on the ground; pants on the ground.
> Lookin' like a fool with your pants on the ground.

Each officer in turn presented me with an old belt or pair of suspenders. How thoughtful.

Once the laughter had subsided, Captain Short addressed the group with a grim face. "Officer Williams, I gave you explicit instructions to go home and stay there. You disobeyed a direct order."

Silence pervaded the room.

I sat waiting for the axe to fall.

"I would have been disappointed if you had done anything else. Congratulations, Walt."

The room burst into applause. Even the captain couldn't resist harassing the old man.

After a brief meeting, the rest of the squad was dismissed to their regular patrol duties. The captain asked Ox and me to stay behind.

"I have a special assignment for the two of you. The body of an old man was found this morning propped up against a tree in a small neighborhood park on Oak Street. He had sustained a massive head wound that was most likely the cause of death. There was no identification on the body, so right now he's a John Doe. Looks like some homeless guy was in the wrong place at the wrong time.

"I'd like you to go to the morgue, find out what you can, canvass the area, and see if you can ID the guy. Maybe someone in the neighborhood heard something."

There are just some places that I avoid like the plague. High on my list are hospitals and nursing homes, but the morgue is at the top of the list.

Each has their unique odor that makes my blood run cold, but the morgue is the worst.

We stopped at the front desk and asked for Dr. Morton Dull, or "Morty," as he preferred to be called.

The small, bald doctor entered through a swinging door.

"Well, if it isn't the Dynamic Duo. What can I do for you today?"

I was surprised that our reputation had reached the recesses of the morgue. I guess celebrity has its perks.

Ox was holding his nose, so I replied, "Captain Short sent us over about the old man that was brought in this morning."

"Ah. I wondered how long it would take before someone showed up. This is a weird one."

"How so?"

"Looks like the old guy died of a shark bite."

"Come again?"

That probably would have been a normal conversation if we were in a morgue in California or Florida, but certainly not in the heart of the great Midwest.

"I was cleaning the head wound and found some fragments of a bone-like material. My analysis showed that they were chips from the teeth of a great white shark."

That got Ox's attention. "Were there other wounds on the body?"

"Nope. Just the massive head wound with the tooth fragments. But I did find this." He handed us a crumpled piece of paper. "It was stuffed in his mouth."

We looked at the paper and saw two words inscribed. "*Mano nuha.*"

Ox stared at the strange words. "Any idea what that means?"

"Not a clue," I replied. But the words had a familiar ring.

"I know there is usually massive blood loss with a head wound. Was there a lot of blood at the scene?"

"No. Clean as a whistle. The attack obviously happened elsewhere, and he was transported to the park."

I handed the crumpled paper back to Morty. "Was there anything else found on the body that could help identify the victim?"

"No, nothing."

Then came the moment I had been dreading.

Ox sighed and said, "I guess we'd better take a look at the body."

We followed Morty into the frigid, smelly bowels of the morgue. Our John Doe was laid out on an autopsy table and covered with a sheet. Carefully, Morty pulled the sheet away, revealing the cold, gray corpse.

"That's no homeless guy!" I gasped. "That's Uncle Ray!"

I called the captain and told him what we knew at that point. Knowing the identity of our victim and his ties to the Hawaiian exhibit, Captain Short sent us to the Nelson Art Gallery.

We stopped at the front desk and asked to speak to a representative from the History and Culture of the Ancient Hawaiians exhibit. Soon a young man in his late twenties approached us with his hand extended.

"Aloha. My name is Buddy Kalakoa. How may I help you?"

Both Ox and I winced at the same time. This was not going to be pleasant.

Ox had been down this sad road before and took the lead. "Are you related to Raymond Kalakoa?"

"Yes, he's my grandfather. Is everything okay? I haven't seen him yet this morning."

"Is there somewhere we can talk in private?"

A look of concern came over him as he led us to a small private office.

"Mr. Kalakoa, I'm afraid we have some bad news. Your grandfather was found this morning in a small park about a half-mile from here. He had been murdered. I'm so sorry."

"*Auwe, Kupuna Kane.*" He moaned and slumped into a chair.

I gave him a moment to regain his composure and asked, "When did you last see your grandfather?"

"At supper. It was a beautiful, warm evening, and he said he wanted to take a walk before retiring. I haven't seen him since. How did he die?"

"We were hoping you could help us with that. He had been struck in the head, and fragments of shark's teeth were found in the wound."

"Oh, *leiomano!*"

"Excuse me?"

"*Leiomano.* It is an ancient Hawaiian war club made of Koa wood embedded with shark's teeth."

The minute he said it, I remembered seeing one in Uncle Ray's exhibit.

I pulled the slip of paper found in Uncle Ray's mouth and handed it to Buddy. "Do you recognize these words?"

He looked at the paper, and a shudder of fear racked his body.

"*Mano nuha*. It means that the shark is angry. I was afraid of this."

I could see the fear in his eyes. "What does that mean? Angry at what?"

"In order for this to make any sense, you have to understand the beliefs of our forefathers. To them, *Mano*, the shark, was our brother. It was he who led the early seafarers from Polynesia to Hawaii. He was a god, of sorts."

Ox was confused. "So why is he angry?"

"Because we have taken holy things from the sacred ground."

"Are you talking about the exhibit?" I asked.

"Yes. The artifacts were found in a burial cave on a sheer cliff face inside the Haleakala Crater. They were the possessions of very powerful *alii*, or chiefs, and had been hidden there for centuries. It was forbidden that anyone even know the whereabouts of these things, let alone remove them."

"Then why were they taken out of the tomb?"

"There are those among my people who want to share the culture and history of our forefathers with the world, but they do so at the risk of angering the gods."

"Go on."

"It is said that the great volcanoes that formed our islands, the home of Pele, the goddess of fire, are sacred, and those who take from the sacred land shall be visited with the curse of Pele."

"Do you believe this is true?"

"What I know to be true is that over the years, many tourists have ignored the warnings and have taken rocks from the mountain as souvenirs. The Hawaii tourist bureau has received many a box of rocks from distraught tourists, begging that the rocks be returned to remove the curse."

Ox was having difficulty following Buddy's story. "But to your knowledge, no one has been bludgeoned with a war club?"

"No, but it is one thing to take a rock and quite another to disturb the resting place of the *alii*. In ancient times, it was forbidden for even the shadow of a commoner to fall upon a chief. Such an offense was punishable by death, often with such a club."

"Wow. That seems awfully harsh," I said.

"You have to understand that my people had traveled three thousand miles to a new land. They were able to prosper because everyone respected the *kapu*, the strict social order that made their survival possible. Those who didn't were killed."

I should have been more sensitive, but I blurted out, "So other than the angry gods, can you think of anyone else who might want your grandfather dead?"

"Please do not mock our beliefs."

"I apologize. I didn't mean to offend."

"Yes, there are those who do not believe as my grandfather did. There are many of my people who long to return to the ancient ways before the white man took everything away. It is they who warned that to remove the sacred things would anger our *aumakua*."

The mention of the word *aumakua* got my attention. It was the word Uncle Ray used when he gave me the tiny lizard.

"Tell me about this *aumakua*."

"All things in nature are our brothers. We were all created by Wakea and Papa. Each of us has a special connection with one of our brothers in nature. For some, it may be a shark; for another it may be a sea bird. We are encouraged to form a bond with our *aumakua* to help guide us through life."

I pulled the black obsidian lizard from my pocket.

Buddy stared in disbelief. "Where did you get that? It has been in my family for years."

I told him the story of our encounter with his grandfather and shared my experience with the tiny lizard the day of Maggie's abduction.

"There is great *mana* in this *aumakua*. My grandfather knew much of the old ways and had far greater understanding than I will ever have. You would be wise to heed his words. Did he say more?"

"He said that Maggie was to be called Hualani and that I was to be called Kamamalu. Does that mean anything to you?"

Again Buddy sat in shocked disbelief.

"Roughly translated, Hualani means 'child of a chief,' and Kamamalu means 'protector.'"

"He also said that his homeland was calling to us, that we wouldn't understand now, but the day would come."

"It is my belief that all things happen for a reason. It is no coincidence that you came to my grandfather's lecture. He was led by the spirits of our ancestors to speak to you and give you *mo'o'ala*. It is no coincidence that it is you who have been sent to avenge his death. You have been chosen by the gods. It is a great honor and responsibility."

Buddy Kalakoa's words played in my mind as we left the gallery.

Why did Uncle Ray have to die?

What does all this have to do with Maggie and me?

Is there really no such thing as coincidence?

What if we hadn't gone to the gallery that day?

If I was confused, I could only imagine what Ox was thinking.

Finally, on the way back to the station, he muttered, "Partner, I think we just stepped into some deep shit."

"Amen to that."

⚖

Later that evening, Maggie was devastated when I told her of Uncle Ray's tragic death. She too had felt a connection with the old man.

I had not, as yet, shared the story of the role that the tiny lizard had played in her rescue. In retrospect, in the cold light of day, the whole thing had seemed so improbable. After my visit with Buddy Kalakoa, I figured she should hear the whole story.

Maggie is a modern girl and, like me, has a rather skeptical attitude toward folklore and superstition, but I could see that she was visibly shaken as I recounted my experience with the *aumakua*.

I hesitated to bring up the next topic that was on my mind, but after all, I had promised, "No secrets."

"Do you remember telling me how you felt a connection to some of the places that Uncle Ray showed in his slides?"

"Indeed I do. It was a kind of déjà vu sensation. I've thought about it several times in the last few days."

"Try not to freak out when I tell you this."

"There's more?"

"Remember when Uncle Ray said that you were to be called Hualani?"

"Yes, it's beautiful, isn't it?"

"Well, the literal translation means 'child of a chief.'"

"Walt, now you are freaking me out. There is absolutely nothing in my heritage that I am aware of that has any connection to anything Hawaiian."

"Hey, don't kill the messenger. I'm just telling you what he said."

"He also said that his homeland would be calling us. What do you suppose that means?"

"Right now, I don't have a clue, but like Buddy, I don't believe in coincidences. Something tells me there is going to be more of Hawaii in our future."

The next morning, we learned at squad meeting that the investigation of Uncle Ray's death had been taken out of our hands and assigned to Homicide.

When it was thought that the victim was just an old homeless dude, the case had been assigned to a couple of grunt cops. As soon the brass heard that the victim was a dignitary of sorts, it was handed over to the "real cops."

The investigation had taken on a "celebrity" status, and the headlines in the *Kansas City Star* pronounced Uncle Ray "an ambassador of goodwill for the Hawaiian people." We also learned that with his untimely death, the traveling exhibit would be shut down.

According to Ronald Kalakua, younger brother of the victim, who was now in charge of the exhibit, "The artifacts will be carefully packed and shipped to the Bishop Museum in Honolulu, where they will become a permanent exhibit for all to enjoy."

Having been stripped of our murder investigation, Ox and I spent the day on our regular patrol duty.

On the one hand, I was disappointed that the brass didn't think the "Dynamic Duo" could handle such a high profile case.

On the other hand, I was relieved. I hoped that maybe fate had taken this Hawaii thing out of my life forever.

I couldn't have been more wrong.

When our shift was over, I hopped into my car and headed down McGee Trafficway, anticipating a quiet evening at home.

I had just pulled into the intersection at Eighteenth Street when an old black Lincoln came barreling through the red light. I jammed on my brakes, but it was too late. The old Lincoln struck me in the right rear quarter panel and spun me around. Neither of us had been speeding, so the impact, while inflicting damage to the cars, was not sufficient to cause either of us bodily injury.

I stepped out of my car and approached the Lincoln. An elderly lady with bright blue hair coiffed high on her head sat dazed behind the wheel.

I tapped on the window. That seemed to jolt her back to reality.

She rolled the window down.

"I'm so sorry! I just don't know where my mind was. I didn't even see the stoplight."

"Are you okay?"

"Yes, I think so," she said as she gingerly felt her body parts. "Am I going to be arrested?"

"Well, that depends. Please tell me you have insurance."

"Oh, absolutely!"

"Well then, let's get these cars out of the intersection, and we can exchange information."

We pulled into a vacant parking lot.

"My name is Lottie Crabtree," she said as she handed me her driver's license.

"Hi, I'm Walter Williams. I'm insured with State Farm. Do you have your insurance card with you?"

"Oh, yes," she exclaimed as she rummaged through her purse. "I used to have State Farm, but I switched to Geico. It saved me a hundred and twenty-eight dollars a year."

Good to know.

"Here it is," she said as she proudly held up her card. "And there's a number here for my agent. Let me give him a call."

I was examining the huge dent in my fender and thinking about all the time and trouble it would take to get it fixed when Lottie connected with her agent.

"Hello, Lawrence, this is Lottie. Yes, it's me again."

Apparently Lottie had been down this road enough times to be on a first-name basis with the agent.

"No, I'm okay, but I think I may have made a little dent in Mr. Williams's car."

Lottie is the mistress of understatement, I thought as I surveyed my crumpled fender.

"Here," she said as she handed me the phone. "He'd like to speak to you."

"This is Walter Williams."

"Hi, I'm Lawrence Grimes. Lottie tells me no one's been injured, so I'm hoping it won't be necessary to call the police."

"Actually, I am the police."

"Oh great! One more incident and Lottie may lose her license. Is there any way we can avoid that? We will, of course, take care of any damage to your car."

I looked over at poor Lottie, who had a death grip on the steering wheel. On the one hand, my cop instinct told me it would probably be better to get Ms. Demolition Derby off the street, but my more compassionate side knew that taking her license would probably put one more nail in her coffin.

Finally, my compassionate side won.

"Okay, how shall we handle this?"

"You have two choices. Tomorrow we can send an adjuster to you to assess the damage to your car, or we have a drive-in location in Argentine that is open until eight o'clock."

"I'll be working tomorrow, so give me the address of your drive-thru, and I'll take care of it tonight."

"Thank you so much. I'm sure Grandma—er, I mean Mrs. Crabtree is very grateful. If you'll give me your information, I'll call it in, and they'll be expecting you."

Well, no wonder she switched to Geico.

Fortunately, the car was drivable, and I headed to Argentine. This is an area on the northwest side of Kansas City, between downtown and the Missouri River. There are homes and businesses in the area, but it is also the hub of the vast railroad network that connects Kansas City with the rest of the continental United States.

As luck would have it, I approached a set of tracks just ahead of an oncoming train. The signal arm dropped, and I was stuck there watching a seemingly endless stream of boxcars and flat cars loaded with eighteen-wheel trailers stacked two deep.

After the train had passed and the signal arm rose, I noted that the street that led to my destination was lined on each side with acres and acres of huge lots, filled with the same trailers that had just passed by. There must have been thousands of them, each one carrying a cargo precious to someone bound for some distant location.

As I passed one of the lots, I noticed smoke curling skyward, but the exact location of the fire was obscured by a row of trailers. Given the industrial nature of the area, I figured it was probably just burning trash. I glanced at my watch, and seeing the late hour, I thought it might be worth a look.

I turned into the lot and rounded the trailer, and the scene before me could have been lifted right out of a Wes Craven horror novel.

Tied to a wooden pole, the figure of a man was barely discernable as the leaping flames consumed his body.

A few feet away, a sign had been erected, and the words, "Kapu. Pele Nuha," were inscribed in a red substance I feared was blood.

I dialed 911 and frantically looked around for something to extinguish the blaze but found nothing. I stood there helpless, watching the remains of some poor soul go up in smoke.

Soon the area was filled with fire trucks and police cars.

I retreated to my car, and as I stood there watching the firemen and officers secure the grisly scene, I realized that I had been clutching the tiny amulet in my pocket.

At that very moment, I noticed for the first time a huge billboard overlooking the lot. My heart skipped a beat as I found myself staring into the eyes of the Geico lizard.

⚖

The next day Ox and I were summoned to Captain Short's office.

I was surprised to see the lead detective from Homicide, but I was even more surprised to see Buddy Kalakoa.

"Come in. I think you know Detective Blaylock, and I believe you've met Mr. Kalakoa."

I shook Buddy's hand and gave a nod to Blaylock, who didn't look at all happy.

Blaylock was a good detective. Ox and I had worked a couple of cases with him, and I thought we were on good terms. I was surprised at his somber expression. Maybe he was just having a bad day.

"Unfortunately," the captain continued, "the body you discovered last evening was that of Ronald Kalakoa."

I looked at Buddy. His head drooped, and I could tell he was doing his best to not lose control.

"I'm so sorry, Buddy."

He nodded.

"Mr. Kalakoa had spent the day supervising the packing of the exhibit and had followed the truck to the rail yard. It was to be loaded on a flat car today and transported to Los Angeles, where it was to be loaded on a container barge and shipped to Honolulu.

"After the trailer was dropped off, he was apparently accosted and—well, you know very well what happened. The trailer was found empty. The artifacts in the exhibit are missing."

"Buddy, I saw the words on the sign. If I remember correctly, *kapu* means forbidden, Pele is the goddess of fire, and *nuha* means angry. I'm guessing all this is connected to your grandfather's death."

"We have angered the gods. We have broken the *kapu*, and they have sought vengeance. The only way to appease the gods is through sacrifice. My grandfather was sacrificed to Mano, the shark, and my uncle to Pele. I will be next."

"Walt," the captain said, "Mr. Kalakoa for some reason believes you may have some special insight into this case and has asked that you be reassigned. We want to honor his wishes, so you and Ox will be working with Detective Blaylock until further notice."

No wonder Blaylock was ticked.

"It will be an honor to work with Mr. Kalakoa. We will do our best."

CHAPTER SIX

Later that evening, after a "Hungry Man" meal was hastily prepared in the trusty microwave, I poured a flute of Arbor Mist and spread my paperwork on the dinette table.

I figured it was time to separate fact from fiction in this most unusual case.

I labeled the first page "fact" and started listing what we knew to be true.

Artifacts that were considered sacred to the ancient Hawaiians had been discovered, removed from their resting place, and placed in a traveling exhibit to be shared with the world.

The caretakers and promoters of this exhibit, the Kalakoa family, had been warned by Hawaiian fundamentalists that they were breaking the *kapu* and had angered the gods.

Subsequently, Uncle Ray had been bludgeoned to death with a Hawaiian war club studded with shark's teeth, and his brother, Ronald, had been set ablaze, both as human sacrifices to appease the angry gods. Buddy Kalakoa, the grandson, now feared for his life.

And finally, the artifacts from the exhibit were taken.

I started to label the second page "fiction," but then the thought occurred to me that fiction really meant "not true," and I wasn't ready to concede that yet. So I scratched that out and wrote "superstition."

Upon further reflection, I decided that what we had encountered went beyond "Don't walk under a ladder," or "Don't let a black cat cross your path." It was definitely more than that.

I finally labeled the second page "unexplained" and started to write.

I was amazed as I analyzed the sequence of events that had transpired over the past week that had brought us to this moment.

It had all started when Maggie started showing houses to the new curator at the gallery. Had he not given her tickets to the Egyptian exhibit, we would never have gone to the gallery that day and met Uncle Ray.

And the words that Uncle Ray spoke to us that day were, of course, shrouded in mystery. What did he mean when he said, "My homeland is calling to you. You have been chosen."?

Only time would tell.

Then I thought of the tiny lizard in my pocket. Uncle Ray had said, "Follow the *mo'o'ala*. He will guide you."

On the day of Maggie's abduction, did I conjure up the exchange plan on my own, or did I have help?

And what caused Lottie Crabtree to run that red light and crumple my fender? It might have just been old age, but had that not happened, I would never have been in the Argentine area that night to find the burning body of Ronald Kalakoa.

And I still get shivers when I remember looking up and seeing the huge lizard staring at me from the billboard high above the burning corpse.

I fancy myself a pretty level-headed guy, and most of the time I'm like Sergeant Joe Friday from the old *Dragnet* show. "Just the facts, ma'am. Just the facts."

But I'm also smart enough to realize that there are forces operating in the universe that are above the understanding of mortal men, and sometimes those forces intervene in our lives.

What are the forces at play that cause the humpback whale to swim thousands of miles from the arctic to the Hawaiian Islands?

What compels the Monarch butterfly and the tiny hummingbird to travel half a continent twice each year?

And what was it that seemed to be leading Maggie and me into—well, into what?

As I sat pondering the two pages I had written, the phone rang, and the voice I heard on the other end was the last person I would have ever expected.

"Walt, we need to talk."

"*Dad?*"

To say that my father and I were estranged would be a stretch. We didn't hate each other. We just didn't have anything to do with each other.

When I was growing up, my male role model was my grandfather. I spent every spare moment on his farm, and to this day I do my best to emulate the qualities that made him dear to me.

My dad, on the other hand, seemed to embody the old saying, "If you can't be a good example, then you'll just have to be a horrible warning."

Now don't get me wrong. Dad was a good provider. While we didn't have a lot of extras, we were comfortable. I never knew Dad to lay a finger on my mother and only on me on those rare occasions when I actually deserved it.

Dad's problem was that he couldn't keep his fingers off of other women. He was quite a ladies' man.

He was an over-the-road trucker, and everyone knew he was like the sailor with a girl in every port.

I grew up in the Eisenhower post-war years. The moral climate in America was certainly different in those days. To be caught in adultery or to conceive a child out of wedlock was sufficient cause to bring shame to an entire family, unlike today, when extra-marital dalliances and pregnancies are commonplace and readily accepted.

Mom was the typical gal from the old country song, "A good-hearted woman in love with a good-timin' man." She bravely looked the other way to spare our family the scandal and disgrace of a divorce. In those days, the woman's place was in the home, and on her own she would have had no way to support us.

Dad would take off for several days at a time on a run to some far-off state, return for a day, and then be on the road again. It wasn't the kind of home life that encouraged male bonding.

I do remember the days that Dad was home.

He loved three things—his cigarettes, his beer, and boxing.

Regular fixtures at our house were the Wednesday and Friday night fights brought to us in black and white by Pabst Blue Ribbon and Gillette. Sugar Ray Robinson was a household name. Dad would pop open his beer, light up a Camel, and spend the evening watching two grown men beat the crap out of each other.

When Mom passed on, I was already out of the nest, and she was the final tie that held our dysfunctional little family together. Dad went his way, and I went mine.

For a while we would call each other on birthdays and holidays, but eventually, I can't actually tell you when, we even stopped doing that.

I heard from a mutual friend that he had taken his retirement from the Teamsters' Union and headed west to Arizona and was living in one of those assisted living places for old folks who can care for themselves.

I knew he was out there somewhere. I guess I just didn't care where.

"Walt, I've got nowhere to go."

"Excuse me?"

"They're kicking me out."

"Who is?"

"Shady Glen."

"What's Shady Glen?"

"It's where I live."

"Why are they kicking you out?"

"Here, talk to Mr. Mayview."

"Hello, Mr. Williams? My name is Leon Mayview. I'm the executive director of the Shady Glen Assisted Living Center. I'm afraid we've had some, uh, issues with your father, and we're going to have to ask him to leave."

"What in the world could an eighty-six-year-old man do that is so terrible?"

"Well, that's the problem. He's not exactly acting his age."

Oh boy! I guess it runs in the family.

"Can you be more explicit?"

"I can, but it's a rather sensitive area."

"Hey, I'm a cop. Don't worry about offending my sensibilities."

"Very well then. Your father is a horny old goat, and it's affecting our entire resident population."

Apparently Dad hadn't mellowed with age.

"How so?"

"Where shall I start? Let's see. Ah, yes. We have no problem with our residents forming personal relation-ships. It's actually quite therapeutic in most cases. But your father has carried it to the extreme. I would imag-ine he has bedded every ambulatory woman at Shady Glen."

"But isn't that one of those personal things between consenting adults?"

"We let it go at that at first, but then things began to escalate."

"Go on."

"One day our orderlies discovered that our regular Friday night bingo had evolved, through your father's influence, into 'bedroom bingo.' The winner of the blackout game got to spend the night with the partner of their choosing."

"May I assume, then, that there was a significant increase in bingo participation?"

"Ah, sarcasm. I can see that the nut didn't fall far from the tree."

"Sorry about that. Please go on."

"We, of course, encourage hobbies such as the chess club and the camera club, but the VP club was just too much."

"VP?"

"Yes, the 'Viagra Poppers.' It was formed by your father, who felt it was his role to educate his peers and encourage the use of the little pill. Their motto is, 'Better living through chemistry.'"

"It's hard to argue with the logic."

"I can see that this going nowhere."

"I guess I don't understand why this couldn't have been handled in house by your staff."

"We certainly tried. It was bad enough when we had to break up a fist fight between two elderly residents over who owned a box of condoms, but it got out of hand when the residents' families got involved."

This couldn't be good.

"Just imagine the outrage when Mrs. Whipple's children found a dildo in her nightstand. They, of course, demanded to know what kind of an operation we were running here."

"Yes, that would be hard to explain."

"The straw that broke the camel's back was when we found your father and Myrtle Mincus in the sitz bath, *au natural.*'"

"Oops! So what are we talking about here?"

"We have terminated your father's residency at Shady Glen. He is paid to the end of the month. He must vacate by then."

"But that's only two weeks away."

"Indeed it is. And none to soon as far as we're concerned."

"So why call me?"

"That was your father's idea. It's of no concern to us as long as he is out of here by the end of the month."

"Swell. Put him back on the phone."

"Walter?"

"Yes, Dad."

"What am I going to do?"

"First things first. Where exactly are you?"

"Sun City, Arizona."

"Give me your contact number, and let me make some calls."

I took his number and booted up my computer. There must be dozens of retirement complexes in Sun City. I'd work on finding one with a vacancy and get him transferred.

Sure enough, there were several pages of listings. I printed the pages and started making calls.

I soon found that each conversation ended the same way.

"Hello, is this the Bear Creek Retirement Village?"

"Indeed it is. How may I help you?"

"Do you have any vacancies?"

"Why, yes, I believe we do. Let me check. By the way, whom would this be for?"

"A Mr. John Williams."

Long pause. "Oh, I'm so very sorry. It looks like our last vacancy was taken this morning."

Hmm. I was beginning to see a pattern.

Then it struck me. They have a "bad dog" list.

When I owned apartments, I was a member of the Landlord's Association. I attended every meeting so I wouldn't miss out on the "bad dog" list.

Unfortunately, there are folks out there who have learned to use and abuse the legal system. They would move into a residence, pay the first month's rent and deposit, and then pay no more. The eviction laws being what they are make it possible for these pikers to remain in the property sometimes for months. When they finally have to leave, they just move on to the next poor landlord who doesn't bother to check references, and the scam starts all over again.

There was a large chalkboard in one corner of the landlord's meeting room, and every month the names of the offending tenants were posted as a warning to the other members. We avoided these "bad dogs" like the plague.

It was soon apparent that my father was on such a list with the retirement complexes.

I gave Maggie a call and told her we needed to talk.

I picked Maggie up at her apartment, and we headed to Mel's Diner for supper.

Mel's is a throwback to the diners of the 1950s—no frou-frou stuff, just real food and lots of it. Everything tastes wonderful because it's cooked in butter. It's what my mom used to call "comfort food," and that's exactly what I needed tonight.

Maggie was shocked when I told her of my conversation. She had never heard me speak of my father and just assumed that he, like my mom, had passed away.

I figured that since we were getting married, she deserved to know about all of the skeletons in my closet.

"So what are you going to do?"

"Why do I have to do anything? I haven't heard from the guy in years. I didn't really like him that much when he was around. I probably wouldn't recognize him if I met him on the street."

"Because he's your father. That's why."

That's not the answer I wanted to hear.

I know people for whom family is everything. They fight and they bicker and they moan and groan, but they can't seem to make it through the day without either calling or seeing each other. For them, the old saying, "Blood is thicker than water," is absolutely true.

But not for me.

I have never understood why people suffer with folks they don't really like just because they're related.

It's probably a character flaw.

"I still don't understand why it's my problem."

"Well, let's start from the beginning. Whether you like it or not, the same blood runs through your veins. How old were you when you left home?"

"Nineteen."

"So for nineteen years, he put a roof over your head and provided food to eat and clothes to wear?"

"Yes, I suppose so."

"And exactly what have you done for him?"

"Well, uh…oh crap, Maggie. I thought you'd understand."

"Did you expect me to tell you to put him adrift on an iceberg like the Eskimos do?"

"Well, no, but—"

"But nothing. He's your father, and if you don't step up to the plate, I'm going to wonder if you're actually the man I thought you were."

See? This is exactly why you shouldn't ask for advice if you don't want to hear the answer.

Earlier in the day, I had been in awe at the forces that seemed to be at play in my life as it applied to the Kalakoa case, but with further reflection, I began to wonder if some power had control over every other aspect of my life as well.

I have five apartments in my building in addition to my own. I rarely have a vacancy. All my tenants except Jerry had been with me for over ten years.

But recently, eighty-six-year-old Mrs. Basset finally gave in to her family and moved into a nursing home.

Was it coincidence or something else that my long-lost father called needing a place to live at the very moment I had a vacant unit?

My father was ecstatic when I called and invited him to live in my building. I mailed him a one-way ticket to Kansas City and made arrangements to pick him up at the airport. The flight landed on time, and I waited patiently at the gate as the passengers deplaned.

When it seemed that everyone had exited the aircraft, I began to worry. Where was my father?

Just then, an elderly gentleman with a full head of wavy gray hair exited the runway—in handcuffs!

I was approached by a stern-looking gent and a very comely flight attendant.

"Mr. Williams?"

"Yes, that's me."

"Is this your father?"

I looked at the old gentleman I hadn't seen in years, and he nodded.

"Yes, I suppose it is."

"My name is Grant, and I'm a federal air marshal. Your father is under arrest for assaulting a flight attendant."

My mouth dropped open, and I just stood there dumbfounded.

Finally, Dad spoke. "All I did was pinch her on the butt."

I held my hand to my head and just stared at the old guy in disbelief. I looked at the attractive flight attendant and thought I detected a smile cross her lips. I reached into my pocket and pulled out my badge.

"If no one was injured, I wonder if maybe we could just chalk this up to senility and turn him over to me as a professional courtesy?" I looked imploringly at the flight attendant.

She gave me a wink. "I think maybe we can work something out if he promises *never* to do it again."

I gave Dad a stern look.

"Absolutely! I promise to behave."

Grant uncuffed him, and they walked away, trying their best not to laugh out loud.

I turned to my father. "Dad!"

"I know. I know. But she was a real looker, wasn't she, son?"

Heaven help me! What have I done?

CHAPTER SEVEN

I felt that it was appropriate to warn the other residents of the building of our new neighbor, and it appeared that they listened. Everyone was waiting on the front porch when we pulled up to the curb.

I made the introductions all around, and the repartee that ensued was like a well-rehearsed play.

Jerry, or "Jerry The Joker" as we call him, thinks he is Kansas City's version of Rodney Dangerfield. His constant patter was driving us all batty until we introduced him to amateur night at the comedy club.

"Hi, Mr. Williams. I understand that you were an over-the-road trucker."

"Yep, I was. But you can call me Big John or just John."

"Well, you know old truckers never die. They just get a new Peterbilt."

"You're right about that, sonny, but I'm still drivin' the old one. You know what Groucho Marx said, 'A man's only as old as the woman he feels.'"

I thought maybe Jerry had met his match.

Then Willie jumped in.

"Why dey call you Big John? You ain't even six feet tall."

"They weren't referring to six feet. They were refer-ring to six inches."

Willie wasn't impressed.

"Only six inches long?"

"No, my friend. Six inches from the ground."

Now Willie was impressed.

Then Dad turned his attention to eighty-three-year-old Bernice Crenshaw.

"Tell me your name again, dear."

"Bernice," she replied coyly.

"Ah, Bernice. A lovely name. I just know we're going to get along famously." With a move that Clark Gable would have envied, he bowed and planted a kiss on Bernice's outstretched hand.

I think the professor summed up what we were all thinking.

"The follies which a man regrets most in his life are those which he didn't commit when he had the opportunity."

Dad certainly made the most of his opportunities.

I took Dad to his apartment, and he unpacked. It didn't take long, and soon we were back on the front porch. Everyone was rocking and talking and just enjoying the balmy day.

On more than one occasion, I had shared stubborn police cases with this austere group and was rewarded with insights that proved invaluable in bringing the case to a successful conclusion.

I perched on the porch rail and brought my friends up to date on the Kalakoa murders and missing artifacts. Everyone sat in silence and let the information sink in.

Finally, the professor spoke.

"I can certainly understand the spiritual overtones of the case, but these atrocities were not committed by the gods. They were committed by zealous men who believe they are appeasing angry gods."

"So what dey gonna do wif de stuff dey stole? Maybe fence it?" Willie asked.

"On the contrary," the professor continued. "Their goal is to return the artifacts to their proper resting place."

"And where is dat?"

"The island of Maui," I said. "They were discovered in a cave in the crater of a dormant volcano."

"So how do they get the stuff back to an island in the Pacific Ocean?" Jerry asked.

"The Kalakoa family had packed it in a container to be shipped to California by rail. From there it was to go to Honolulu by ship, but the container was found empty. It appears it was loaded into another trailer, but we don't have a clue where it went from there."

Dad had just sat there, quietly listening to our exchange. Finally, Dad chimed in, "They couldn't send it by rail. There are too many people who would have to be involved. They would have hired a private contractor with his own tractor to move the trailer to the shipyard in Los Angeles."

"But Dad, there are thousands of eighteen-wheelers on the road. It would be like trying to find a needle in a haystack."

"Not if you know where to look. The most direct route from Kansas City to Los Angeles is I-70 to Cove-Fort, Utah, and then I-15 to Southern California. And there are weigh stations all along the route."

"How does that help us?"

"The trucking industry is heavily regulated, and every driver must carry a logbook. This book *must* be current every time you start or stop. If you don't, you can be fined, and I'm sure these guys don't want to draw attention. The logbook must also list the shipper and commodity being carried, the point of origin, and the destination point. So now, how many rigs leaving Kansas City are going all the way to Los Angeles? You've eliminated a whole lot of needles."

"Anything else?"

"Yep. These guys aren't going to use a big shipping company. Too many questions. They will use an independent guy who works for himself."

"And how can we get a list of these guys?"

"Call my old buddy Tony Mancuso at the union hall."

"Ah, the teamsters."

"You bet. Any guy who has shelled out thirty to forty grand for a Peterbilt or K-Whacker is going to belong to the union."

Sweet! Maybe this old fart had some redeeming qualities after all.

I was fairly confident that the thieves would not hang around Kansas City any longer than necessary, so I called the captain and shared the information gleaned from our front porch session.

He agreed and asked me to take Dad to the union hall and talk to Tony Mancuso.

Dad had been a teamster for forty years before he retired and knew everyone but the new guys. He and Tony went back a long way.

After a round of backslapping, hugging, and catching up, we got down to business. Tony was reluctant, at first, to share the information, but I gently reminded him that it would be a lot less trouble for everyone concerned to share the data informally with me than for us to get a court order and bring in guys from the station to dig into their files.

The teamsters being the teamsters, he finally agreed.

He entered the search parameters in the computer, and soon we had a list of the independent contractors working out of the local union, with names, addresses, and the ID numbers on their tractors.

I faxed the list to the captain, and before the day was over, weigh stations along I-70 and the highway patrols from Kansas City to Utah were on the lookout for our perps. Any independent contractor whose logbook showed K.C. to L.A. was detained while officers searched their trailers for the contraband.

Find the missing artifacts, and we find our killers.

Days passed and dozens of trailers were searched, but we were no closer to finding the missing artifacts than the day they were taken. Either the thieves had slipped through our net by taking back roads around the weigh stations or had gotten word about the searches and were laying low until things cooled off. Either way, we had no idea whether the missing items were still in Kansas City or on a barge headed to Honolulu.

Dad had settled in nicely. I introduced him to Maggie, and he promptly told me, "If I were twenty years younger, we'd be knocking heads over that one, sonny."

This, of course, only endeared him to my sweetie.

Dad had wasted no time. He and Bernice had quickly become an item. I suppose they figured that at their age there was no point in being coy.

One afternoon, I happened to overhear their conversation as they sat swinging side-by-side on the porch.

"Bernice, dear, what is that lovely fragrance you're wearing? It's absolutely divine."

"I hoped you would like it, John. I bought it especially for you."

"Indeed I do."

"Well, you smell very nice yourself. What do you have on?"

"Well, actually, I have a hard on." He grinned. "But I didn't think you could smell it."

I guess they are swingers in more ways than one.

If someone had told me a month before that I'd be double-dating with my father, I would have laughed in their face.

It's absolutely uncanny how life's little twists and turns can change everything in an instant.

But there we were.

Dad, Bernice, Maggie, and I had piled into the car and headed to Oak Grove, about fifteen miles east of Kansas City, to share a meal and drinks at one of our favorite Mexican restaurants. After a hearty meal of chips, salsa, fajitas, and more margaritas than any of us should have imbibed, we decided to call it a day. I was just about to turn on to I-70 when Dad spoke up.

"Got me a problem, sonny. My old bladder has shrunk to about the size of a golf ball, and those margaritas are going right through me. How about we pull into that truck stop and let me drain the main vein?"

"Me too." Bernice giggled. "If I laugh too hard, I'm going to pee my pants."

"Then by all means, we should stop."

I pulled into the big TA truck stop, and the old folks hopped out.

There must have been twenty big rigs lined up side-by-side in the lot. Their drivers were either in the restaurant or had decided to bunk there for the night.

I pulled the list that Tony had given us and started cross-checking the numbers on the cabs with the numbers on our list. Maggie soon grew bored and flipped on the radio to pass the time while we waited for Dad and Bernice to return from their potty break.

I hadn't expected to find any matches, but what else did I have to do?

Then there it was.

I checked and rechecked the numbers and found a match.

I was just about to say something to Maggie when I heard Boy George warbling his hit from 1980, and the words took my breath away, "Karma, karma, karma, karma, karma chameleon."

We looked at each other.

"It just can't be," I whispered.

"How can it not be?"

I hopped out of the car and quietly circled the eighteen-wheeler. No one was around. The pull-down door on the trailer was secured with a padlock.

Everything I had ever learned about police procedure told me to call for backup and do it by the book.

Then I felt the tiny obsidian amulet in my pocket and heard Boy George crooning from my car.

Just a coincidence?

Sorry. I don't believe in coincidences.

Lady Justice often operates in mysterious ways. Who am I to argue?

I popped the lid on my trunk.

Old habits are hard to break. In my landlord days, I carried a toolbox loaded with all kinds of gadgets to deal with apartments and tenants. One of my staple items was a bolt cutter. People mistakenly believe that a padlock is secure and will keep people out of whatever is being locked.

Nothing is further from the truth.

A good, sharp bolt cutter will pop the shackle on a padlock in seconds.

I retrieved my cutter and had just snapped the lock when I heard, "What in tarnation do you think you're doing?"

I had fully expected to see a burly trucker headed my way, but it was just my father.

"Dad! You scared the crap out of me."

I filled him in on what I had found, and we slowly, and as quietly as possible, raised the door on the trailer.

I told Dad to keep an eye out for anyone coming our way and entered the bowels of the trailer to inspect the cargo.

Sure enough, the bill of lading attached to the crates still bore the final destination that Ronald Kalakoa had printed before his death, "Bishop Museum, Honolulu, Hawaii."

"So what are we going to do?" Dad whispered as we huddled by the car.

"I have to call for backup. We can't handle this alone. We have no idea how many there are."

"But what if they come back before your buddies arrive? Are you packing heat?"

Off-duty officers are supposed to be armed at all times, but I just never could get in the habit. Somehow it didn't feel right carrying a revolver on a date. I understand now why they suggest you do it.

I shook my head no.

"Well, great. Then we need to get this thing out of here before they come back."

"What are you talking about?"

"I'm saying that you call your buddies while I get this thing going, and we'll get the hell out of Dodge."

"Can you still drive one of these things?"

"Is a frog's pussy watertight?" was all he replied.

I wasn't exactly up to speed on my amphibian anatomy, but I presumed that was an affirmative answer.

"But the cab is locked. And how would you start it?"

He just shook his head and started feeling under the huge wheel wells.

"Ah. Here it is." He pulled a magnetic key holder from the wheel well.

"Best not to waste any time. Call it in, and I'll head to your precinct."

"I'm coming with you," Bernice squealed. "I've always wanted to ride in one of these."

"Then let's get your cute little butt into the cab."

Dad tucked Bernice into the passenger seat, and soon I heard the rumble as the big diesel engine roared to life.

I called the precinct, and the captain wasn't exactly enthused at my initiative.

"Walt! What in the hell were you thinking? You broke into a truck, hijacked it, and it's now being driven by an eighty-year-old guy and his girlfriend?"

"Uh, yeah. That's pretty much it."

"So where are you now?"

"We're just about to leave Oak Grove and head west on I-70."

"Just terrific! I'll send a couple of black and whites to intercept you and escort you in. Heaven help us."

I looked at Maggie. She just shook her head and rolled her eyes. I had hoped my Lois Lane would be a bit more supportive.

I pulled out of the parking lot with Dad close behind, and we entered the on-ramp to I-70 westbound.

We were clipping along at sixty-five miles an hour, and I thought we were home free when two huge, black SUVs pulled alongside. One of them pulled into the lane directly in front of me, and the other crowded my left side.

We were approaching the exit ramp for Buckner-Tarsney Road, and the passenger in the car to my left pointed to the ramp.

The SUV in front slammed on the brakes, and the guy on the left forced me onto the exit ramp.

I looked in the rearview mirror as I hit my brakes hard and saw Dad barreling toward our rear end. He jammed on his brakes, and I saw the big rig jackknife. The trailer swung dangerously across two lanes of traffic.

We had just barely entered the ramp as Dad went whizzing by. Miraculously, he righted the fishtailing rig as he sped along I-70.

I pulled to the shoulder of the exit ramp, and a stocky Hawaiian guy with a gun ordered us out of the car and into the forward SUV.

I noticed the words inscribed on the front of his T-shirt, "Hawaiian by birth." Then he turned around, and the words, "American by force," were inscribed on the back.

This couldn't be good.

Maggie and I sat in the backseat of the SUV as we sped north on Buckner-Tarsney Road.

"Who are you guys, and why are you doing this?" I asked.

The guy with the gun answered, "We are Kanaka Maoli, and we are simply taking back what is ours."

"What is Kanaka Maoli?"

"We are people of Hawaiian blood. The sacred resting place of our ancestors has been defiled, and we have come to claim the bones of our forefathers and punish those who have angered the gods."

"But how can sharing your culture with the world be a bad thing?"

"I would not expect a *haole* to understand. How you like it if we come to mainland and dig up your Lincoln or Kennedy and carry his bones to our village?"

I hadn't exactly thought of it in those terms.

"So what happens now?"

"You have angered Pele, who has guarded the sacred bones for centuries, and now you must pay. We will not rest until they have been returned."

We rode in silence through the back roads of Eastern Jackson County.

I could feel Maggie shivering, and I held her hand. I wanted to offer her some words of encouragement, but under the circumstances, nothing seemed appropriate.

We turned off a gravel road into a farm field. There were no lights or farmhouses anywhere to be seen. They had picked a remote area far from prying eyes to exact their vengeance and offer their sacrifice.

Two old wooden gateposts stood as silent sentries at the edge of the field. I was bound to one and Maggie to the other.

One of the men carried a five-gallon gas can from the back of one of the SUVs and saturated the ground around each of us.

The four men then gathered in a circle between us, and one of them began to chant in Hawaiian.

Under more favorable circumstances, we would have thoroughly enjoyed the ceremony. I was mesmerized as I listened to the beautiful, lyrical phrasing that was totally foreign to us.

The chant was long and drawn out, and I could only imagine the words of supplication that were being offered to their gods.

As the chant droned on, a different sound broke the silence of the night. It sounded like the distant rumbling of an approaching storm.

The sound grew in intensity, and soon the words of the chant were no longer audible.

The ground began to shake, and the Hawaiians looked around in terror, wondering if they had invoked a personal appearance from Pele herself.

But it was not the gods who were approaching. It was the headlights of two-dozen massive eighteen-wheelers.

The first big rig crashed through the rusty barbed wire fence with gears grinding and diesel smoke billowing from the exhaust. Each rig followed in turn, and soon the huge trucks, much like Indians circling a wagon train, surrounded us. I could see flashing lights outside the circle, and soon officers from the highway patrol, the sheriff's office, and the K.C. police department flooded the area.

A sheriff's deputy cut our bindings, and Maggie ran into my arms sobbing. This was the second time in a month that she had been abducted. I silently wondered how much more she could endure.

As I stood there holding the most precious thing in my life, I saw an old dude climb painfully from the cab of one of the trucks and come hobbling in my direction.

"Dad! How on earth…?" I pointed to the wall of steel around us.

"Simple, sonny. CB radio. I was on the horn the minute we pulled out of the parking lot."

"You guys still use those things?"

"You bet we do. I couldn't stop in time to make the exit ramp, so my good buddy Earl, who was right behind, kept an eye on you till I found the next exit. By the time I caught up, we had us a convoy."

C.W. McCall would have been proud.

Who knew that Lady Justice could drive a big rig?

Suddenly a frail little figure burst into the circle and grabbed Dad around the waist. She was out of breath, and her face was flushed. All Bernice could muster was, "Man, that was a real hoot!"

CHAPTER EIGHT

As I reflected on the events of the past month, I was amazed at the dramatic shift my life had taken.

Somehow, not only my life but the lives of all those around me, including a father whom I hadn't seen in years, were drawn into the vortex swirling around the Kalakoa family and the ancient Hawaiian artifacts.

Uncle Ray had said that Maggie and I had been chosen, but I had nearly lost her twice since his proclamation. Each time I felt a renewed urgency to take her as my wife. I couldn't bear the thought of being without her.

Unlike my dad, who seemed to enjoy his life as a geriatric Casanova, the thought of being out there again was even more frightening than the idea of being alone.

Once again, the guys at the precinct couldn't pass up the opportunity to harass the old man. I had taken a day off to decompress, but on the morning of my return, I was bombarded with wieners and marshmallows, just in case I wanted to host another bonfire.

To an outsider, this constant haranguing might seem cruel and insensitive. But since no one was actually hurt, the act of poking fun at and ridiculing the situation seems to take the power away from what could have been a tragic event.

I can live with that.

I learned that our four abductors were in custody and were to be arraigned on charges of murder, kidnapping, and grand theft. The artifacts were again secure and were awaiting transport to the West Coast, this time under guard.

The captain informed me that Buddy Kalakoa had requested that Maggie and I drop by the art gallery. He wanted to thank us personally for our role in reacquiring the artifacts.

I thanked the captain but silently wondered if there might be more. I wasn't convinced that our Hawaiian adventure had come to an end.

I picked Maggie up after work, and we headed to the art gallery. We found Buddy sitting at his desk. After the perfunctory greetings and words of thanks, I got down to business.

"Buddy, did you know those guys who did those horrible things?"

"I knew of them. They are part of a Hawaiian sovereignty group who have established a village near Waimanolo in the Koolau Mountains on the island of Oahu."

"What do you mean by sovereignty?"

"You have to understand some basics of Hawaiian history. Our form of government was a monarchy before the white man came. Much like the history of your American Indian, our lands were taken, our people were killed, and our government was overthrown. Today only twenty percent of the land is owned by people of Hawaiian blood."

"So what are their goals?"

"Their ultimate goal is to reestablish the Hawaiian monarchy and form an independent government."

"Are you talking about seceding from the United States?"

"Yes."

"The travel posters call Hawaii the 'Land of Aloha,' sunny beaches, mai tais, and hula girls."

"That's the hype, but nothing could be further from the truth. That's the corporate spin, but all that glitz is man-made and has nothing to do with the 'real' Hawaii."

"Do all your people feel that way?"

"Most Hawaiians wish things were different, but there's no turning back the clock. Money and power rule. Think of the defense installations, the hotels, shopping centers, and the multimillion-dollar homes on the beach. It is what it is, and most of us realize we just have to make the best of a tragic situation."

"Most, but not all."

"Yes, there is a small but very vocal group who want to return to the old ways. I understand, and I am sympathetic. But I am also a realist, and I know they are fighting a losing battle. Rather than alienate the rest of the world, our goal is to share the history of our beautiful culture and preserve it for future generations. That is the purpose of our traveling exhibit."

"Well," Maggie chimed in, "it certainly opened our eyes. We knew nothing of Hawaiian history until we heard your grandfather's lecture. He was a special man."

"Indeed he was. He had very powerful *mana* and was able to see things most men cannot see. Take you, for example."

"Me?"

"Yes, he said you were to be called Hualani. The literal translation means 'child of a chief.' I became curious, so I did some research. My people are very big on genealogy. I have heard of a man in the village by Waimanolo who has seven generations tattooed on his leg."

"So what does that have to do with me?"

"Shortly after the discovery of the islands, missionaries from New England came to the islands to convert the heathen idol worshipers to Christianity. Unfortunately, the white man brought more than the gospel. They also brought diseases like smallpox and measles, from which the islanders had no immunity. Eventually, over ninety percent of the Hawaiian population died."

"Again, what does that have to do with me?"

"You are related to one of the early missionaries."

"Wha ... ? How do you know that?"

"I traced your genealogy. A missionary came to the islands and eventually married the daughter of an *alii*, a chief. They conceived a daughter, but shortly after, the mother died of smallpox. The grieving father returned to New England with his daughter. That young girl was your great-great-grandmother. You have Hawaiian blood flowing in your veins. You are Hualani, child of a chief."

"So what is the significance of all that?" I asked. "And what exactly did Uncle Ray mean when he said she had been chosen?"

"I wish I could tell you. Uncle Ray knew things I cannot begin to know. But I know this—the two of you have a destiny to fulfill in my homeland. Hawaii will call and you will come."

Maggie and I were silent as we drove away from the gallery. A thousand different things were playing in our minds.

Buddy had thanked us profusely and said that *when*, not *if*, we came to the islands to call him first. He had relatives on every island that would be our hosts and guides. Apparently, our part in saving the artifacts had been shared with the folks back home, and we were heroes of sorts.

Maggie spoke first. "I'm trying to get my head around all of this, but it just doesn't compute. So what if I have a tiny bit of Hawaiian blood? All of our families came from somewhere. If you look far enough into anyone's history, there will be a tie to some other part of the world. Why is this important? Why me?"

I thought about making light of the situation, just blowing it off as so much superstition, but then I thought of the little lizard in my pocket.

"I wish I had an easy answer, but I don't. Neither of us asked for any of this. We were just living our lives, and somehow we got dragged into this whole Hawaii thing. But now the artifacts are safe, and the perps are in jail. Maybe our part in this saga is finished."

Maggie turned and gave me the look. "You don't believe that any more than I do, but thanks for trying."

"All I know is this—we have to go back to living our normal lives, and whatever happens, happens. I also know that I love you, and I want you to be my wife. I want to marry you *now*!"

"Define 'now.'"

"As soon as possible."

"So are we headed to the courthouse to find a judge?"

"You know what I mean."

"No, I don't. Tell me, Mr. Wedding Planner, what date did you have in mind? Where is this event to take place? Who are we going to invite? Will we have a reception? Will this be a civil or religious ceremony? Who will be doing the catering? What are we going to wear? Are we going on a honeymoon? Where are we going to live after we're hitched? Well?"

Silence.

I think I realized why I'd never married before.

"Does it really have to be that complicated?"

"Which of the things I just mentioned do you think we can eliminate?"

I couldn't think of any.

"You're the bride. Have you been thinking about any of this stuff?"

"Of course I have. I knew you wouldn't."

"So what did you decide?"

Wrong question.

"*Decide?* This isn't *my* decision. It's *our* decision. If you want to get married, you have to participate."

"Maybe I phrased that wrong. What ideas have you come up with that we can discuss?"

"Nice save, but don't think you've fooled me even a little bit."

I had expected a laundry list of ideas, but I was surprised by her response.

"I just don't know. This is supposed to be a special day, a first time for both of us. On the one hand, a simple civil ceremony doesn't seem like quite enough, but a big church wedding seems inappropriate for two people our age. I don't want a huge crowd of people, but who do you not invite and hurt their feelings? We could just have a small private ceremony and then invite everyone to a big reception. I just don't know."

She had obviously given the subject more thought than I had. I knew any contribution from me at that point would only shed more light on my lack of fore-thought, so I chose to remain silent.

We pulled up in front of my building, and a small congregation had gathered on the front porch.

Willie, the professor, Jerry, Dad, and Bernice were rocking and chatting, and I knew Maggie and I didn't have a snowball's chance of running this gauntlet without a prolonged interrogation of our day's events.

I took Maggie's hand and headed for the porch.

"Let's get this over with," I said.

We shared an abbreviated account of our meeting with Buddy Kalakoa, who had asked that we send his thanks to Dad for his part in the recovery of the artifacts.

Dad was his usual self, and his response was not unexpected.

"Glad I could help, sonny. It gave me a chance to do one of the two things I love doing the most, driving and—"

"Uh, yeah, Dad. We get the picture."

"Since you two made it through that mess without becoming shish kabobs, when you going to get hitched?"

We just looked at each other.

I got the we-might-as-well-tell-them look, and we spilled our guts regarding all the uncertainties of our upcoming nuptials.

It was then that I remembered a quote from a *Dirty Harry* movie: "Opinions are like assholes. Everybody's got one."

Sure enough, everyone on the porch had an opinion.

Not only did they have opinions as to why and whether we should get married, but they were also eager to share some of their personal insights into the institution itself.

Someone pointed out that marriage was a good thing. Statistics show that married men live longer. Dad countered by declaring that not to be true. It just seems longer.

Bernice, who dumped her husband, said that if it weren't for marriage, men would spend their lives thinking they had no faults at all. I suspect that by the time he left, Bernice's husband was well aware of his.

The professor, always the philosopher, shared that love is blind but marriage is an eye-opener.

Jerry said that if we decided to take a honeymoon, he hoped it would be like a dining room table—four bare legs and no drawers.

But it was Willie's comment that gave us the most to think about.

"Wot you two need to get married fo' anyway? Ain't you happy now?"

As we climbed the stairs to my apartment, with the comments of our friends fresh in my mind, I was painfully aware of why nothing ever gets settled in committees.

We were just plain tuckered out. We had been kidnapped, almost roasted, and saved by a horny old man and his eighty-six-year-old bimbo. My sweetie had been told that she was a Hawaiian princess with a destiny to fulfill, and we had just been grilled by the front porch inquisition. Neither of us wanted to think about weddings or work or mysteries of any kind. We just wanted to veg out.

We ordered a pepperoni lovers pizza from Dominos, popped open a bottle of Arbor Mist, and hunkered down in front of the TV, prepared to lose ourselves in the oblivion of the silver screen.

"Go to the Turner Classic Movie channel," Maggie suggested. "I need something old and sweet and not too exciting. Kind of like you."

Wow! What a compliment.

I flipped through the channels and found TCM. The credits for the next movie were just rolling. We were just in time to see *Blue Hawaii*.

We were mesmerized as Elvis sang and danced through the 1961 classic.

A tear rolled down Maggie's cheek as the King sang "Can't Help Falling In Love." That was the song I did for Maggie on the night I proposed to her.

At the end of the movie, Elvis and Joan Blackman, who played Maile Duvall, were married in one of the most beautiful settings we had ever seen. They strolled down a path lined with stately palm trees and boarded a raft, which carried them along a lagoon surrounded by a lush tropical garden.

When the movie concluded, we both sat quietly, but our thoughts were on the same wavelength.

Finally, I said, "Are you thinking what I'm thinking?"

"If you're thinking about getting married in Hawaii, I probably am."

"Really? You would actually consider that?"

"Are you kidding? What woman wouldn't be thrilled to be swept off to a tropical paradise to marry the man of her dreams?"

"It would solve a lot of our logistical problems, like where to have the ceremony, who to invite, what to wear. I have to admit, as much as I want to marry you, I just wasn't excited about all the hoopla involved in making it happen. Now this I can get excited about."

"It just feels right, doesn't it?"

I was about to reply in the affirmative when I noticed the credits rolling across the screen for the next Turner Classic Movie.

A chill shook my body, and the hairs stood at attention on the back of my neck when I saw that Richard Burton, Ava Gardner, and Deborah Kerr were about to star in Tennessee Williams's *The Night of the Iguana*.

So how does one begin to plan a Hawaiian wedding? The Internet, of course.

I Googled *Blue Hawaii* and discovered that the beautiful wedding scene had been filmed at the Coco Palms Resort on Kauai. Upon further investigation,

I was disappointed to learn that the resort had been destroyed in 1992 by Hurricane Iniki and was the only resort on the island that had never been rebuilt.

Then, in the next article on the page, I found a listing for a Coco Palms wedding, and the contact person listed was a Larry Rivera.

Wait a minute! How could some guy offer a wedding in a resort that had been blown away? Probably just a scam to get some poor sucker's tourist dollars.

Then it occurred to me. Buddy Kalakoa said that if we ever came to Hawaii to give him a call. Why not?

I called Buddy's cell and told him what Maggie and I had decided to do. I shared with him our disappointment with the Coco Palms and what I had discovered on the Internet.

I was surprised at his answer.

"Not a problem, bro. Uncle Larry will take care of you."

"Uncle Larry?"

"Sure. I told you I have relatives on every island. Larry Rivera is my mother's cousin."

"How can he conduct marriages in a place that's been blown away?"

"You need to understand Larry's story. He was a young employee at the Coco Palms when *Blue Hawaii* was being filmed. He and Elvis became lifelong friends, and eventually Larry and his family became the feature attraction at the resort before the hurricane. Only a handful of people are allowed on the grounds, and Larry is one of them. They have preserved the lagoon and bridge you saw in the movie as well as the small chapel. That's where the weddings are conducted."

"So it's legit."

"Absolutely. Larry is a legend on Kauai. He is a songwriter and performer, and you will love his beautiful Hawaiian melodies. When you contact him, just tell him that I referred you. You'll get the royal treatment. Also, let me know your itinerary on the islands, and I will set you up with some guides."

See? It's not what you know, but who you know.

Maggie was thrilled when I shared the news with her.

Now it was time to get down to business.

So many decisions. When did we want to go? How long should we stay? What islands should we visit? How would we get there?

Then another thought occurred to us. Were we going alone, or were we going to share this special event in our lives with someone dear to us?

We thought long and hard on that one.

We would certainly be more flexible if it was just the two of us, but in the end we didn't want to be alone. We wanted to share the experience with loved ones who had stood by us through the years and had been willing to put themselves in harm's way to protect us.

Who better than Willie and Mary?

It would cost a bundle to bring them along, but RCA Records had given me a reward for recovering the lost Elvis tapes. I couldn't think of a better way to spend it.

We broke the news to Mary first. Her eyes lit up like a little kid's on Christmas morning.

"Really? Me? To Hawaii? With you?"

Maggie took Mary's hand. "I'd be honored to have you stand up with me at our wedding."

A tear ran down Mary's face. "I always dreamed of going there but never figured I'd ever get to do it." Long pause. "I always wanted one of those fancy drinks with the little umbrellas. Do you think we could get one?"

"As many as you want," I replied. "Well, within limits, of course."

"And a grass skirt. I want a grass skirt and one of those coconut shell bras."

I took a look at Mary's ample bosom and silently wondered if coconuts came in size forty-four double D.

"And the sunsets. I've seen pictures of the Hawaiian sunsets. They're *so* beautiful."

Then the tears came again. She grabbed us and hugged us tight.

I think we made her day.

Willie was a different story.

He had lived most of his life on the streets in a hand-to-mouth existence. I doubt he had ever taken a real vacation. I thought he would, like Mary, be excited with the prospect of traveling to exotic places.

His first question was, "How we gonna get der?"

"We'll fly, of course."

"In a plane?"

"Is there any other way?"

"I don't know. I ain't never been on a plane."

I was in shock. Here was a guy who had rubbed shoulders with the worst life had to offer, a guy who had barreled into a gunman head first to save my life, and he was afraid to fly.

"Did you know that statistically you have a much better chance of getting hit by a car than dying in a plane crash?"

Willie wasn't impressed by my logic.

"Yeah, but dat's down here. Not way up der." He looked toward the heavens.

"Maggie and Mary and I will all be with you."

I guess the thought of all of us dying together wasn't much of a comfort.

"I don' know, Mr. Walt. I wanna go but…" He saw the look of disappointment in my eyes. "How come you want me to go? Is it really dat special to you?"

"I want you to go because you're my best friend, and I want you to be the best man at my wedding. It would mean a lot to me."

He didn't say a word, but I could see the wheels turning.

Finally, he said, "Okay, I'll go. Maybe I can get in dat 'Mile High Club.'"

I guess we each have our own way of overcoming our fears.

CHAPTER NINE

I was elated when we finally agreed upon the Hawaiian wedding. I figured all of the nagging questions that had plagued both of us were behind us. Instead, a whole new set of decisions had to be made.

Why does life have to be so complex?

One burning question was what we were going to do when we returned.

We would board the Hawaii-bound aircraft as two singles living in separate quarters, but we would return as a married couple to live—where?

Maggie had a small, one-bedroom condo on the Plaza that was barely big enough for her.

My apartment had two bedrooms but only one bath and a small kitchen.

I couldn't help thinking of Maggie's occasional overnighters and our friendly jousts as we sparred for spitting rights into the sink.

Anything was tolerable in the short term, but how was I going to feel after a month of waiting for Maggie to conclude her extended throne duties?

The professor's words kept playing over in my mind: "Love is blind, but marriage is a real eye-opener."

I had never been married or even lived with another woman, but I was sixty-seven years old, and I hadn't just fallen off of the turnip truck.

Jokes such as, "My wife and I were happy—then we got married," abound.

Unfortunately, the humor is founded in reality. I personally know of couples that blissfully dated for years but couldn't make the marriage work.

Sometimes I wonder about the old saying, "Be careful what you wish for. You might just get it."

Sometimes things that look so good on the surface aren't all they're cracked up to be.

Maggie and I love to watch *American Idol*. We were thrilled when we learned that the summer tour would have a stop in St. Louis. We bought tickets, booked a hotel, and drove across the state anxiously anticipating an evening enjoying the music of our favorite Idols.

Nothing could have been further from the truth.

We had purchased good seats, but that turned out to be a waste of money because no one sat. The sell-out crowd stood from the first note to the very last. Of course, they couldn't just stand. They had to scream and wave their arms as well. I came to hear Katharine McPhee, but all I could hear was the crazy woman behind me. The final indignity came when the fat kid sitting next to me dropped his cotton candy in my lap.

I didn't want my marriage to turn into my Idol experience.

Also, having learned that it is usually prudent to discuss such weighty matters with your partner, I broached the subject with Maggie.

Understandably, she had been concerned as well.

But once again fate intervened in our lives and offered a solution to our problem.

Mrs. Nugent, who had lived in 1B for years, decided to join Mrs. Basset, who had recently vacated 1A, in the assisted living center.

With a little arm-twisting, I convinced Jerry to move from 3B to 1B, thus leaving the whole third floor available for my new bride and me.

I contacted a remodeling contractor who promised to convert the two two-bedroom apartments into a spacious three-bedroom, two-bath with an office during the three weeks we were to be away.

Problem solved.

Finally, after days of agonizing over airline schedules, hotel reservations, and car rentals, it was time to go.

Vince had the only vehicle big enough to haul all four of us and our luggage, and he volunteered to take us to the airport. Maggie had spent the night so that she, Willie, and I could be picked up at my apartment. We heard the *toot* from his horn, grabbed our bags, and headed downstairs.

Knowing my friends as I do, I should have expected what was awaiting us on the front porch, but it took us totally by surprise.

Dad, Bernice, Jerry, and the professor had set up a card table with a small cake and champagne.

Dad spoke first. "We may not be able to be at the big shindig, but we sure as hell aren't going to let you get away without a proper send-off."

With that, he popped the cork and poured the bubbly.

He raised his glass. "A toast to my son and his lovely bride. First, let me say how proud I am to have a son like you. I wasn't a good dad, and I know it. You probably turned out better than if I was around. I weren't a good husband, neither, so I hope you learned from my mistakes and take good care of this special lady."

After his brief lapse into morality, Dad reverted to his usual self. "At least I didn't name you Sue," he said. He proceeded to tie tin cans to Vince's back bumper and placed a "Getting Hitched" sign in the back window.

Then came the airport jokes.

The professor blessed us with the Confucius classic, "Man who fly upside down have big crack up."

Jerry, not to be outdone, droned, "A vulture was boarding an airplane with two dead raccoons. He was stopped at the gangway by a flight attendant. 'I'm sorry, sir; only one carrion per passenger.'"

Once the toasting, joking, hugging, and crying were dispensed with, we stowed the bags and headed to the Three Trails to pick up Mary.

As expected, she was waiting for us on the porch with—yikes!—four huge suitcases.

"Mary! What's all of this?"

"It's my stuff. We're gonna be gone for three weeks, and I gotta have my stuff."

She had more than the rest of us put together.

"One bag, Mary. That's it."

"Hell, I can't get my underwear in just one bag."

I looked at Maggie. "This is your department. I don't know about women's things, but we've gotta have a shakedown."

Maggie and Mary took the bags inside, and after a prolonged struggle peppered with language that would have made a sailor blush, they emerged with one suitcase that probably weighed eighty pounds. I decided at that point to utilize the curbside check-in. The skycaps aren't as fussy about weight if the tip is big enough.

Willie had been unusually quiet, and I noticed on the forty-five-minute drive to the airport that he sat rigid, fists clenched, staring straight ahead. Instead of enjoying the trip to a tropical paradise, he was experiencing what I would imagine a convict would feel on his way to the gas chamber.

We arrived at the airport, and after a bit of wrangling with the skycap and a huge tip, we made our way to the gate.

Naturally, the line extended down the hallway.

I took this opportunity to educate our novice flyers on the security procedures instituted after 9/11.

"You means I got to undress befo' de let me on de plane?" Willie said.

"Well, not everything, just your belt and shoes and anything metal in your pockets."

Maggie and I went first to show Willie and Mary how it was done.

No problems.

Willie was next, and I heard him mutter, "Dis is worse dan when I went to visit Louie de Lip in county lockup."

Three down, and one to go.

Mary placed her enormous purse on the conveyor and stepped through the metal detector.

Brring! The detector lit up like a Christmas tree.

"Ma'am, would you step over here please?"

Mary followed the slender TSA matron to a small cubicle.

"Please stand on those footprints and raise your arms."

So far so good. Mary hadn't threatened anyone yet.

The TSA gal grabbed a wand and started running it over Mary's body. No problem until she put the thing between Mary's legs.

"Hey, girlfriend. You making a porno movie or something? Hey! Get that thing out of my—"

"Sorry, ma'am."

"Walt, this skanky bitch is poking my doodah with that dildo!"

"It's okay, Mary. She's just doing her job."

The TSA gal ran the wand up Mary's torso. The wand came to life as it passed over Mary's chesticles.

"Ma'am, do you have anything metal on your body?" She laid the wand down and started feeling around Mary's protruding breasts.

"Walt! Now she's feeling me up." Then she addressed the TSA matron. "Of course I got on something metal. You don't think these babies perk out like that on their own, do you? You're feeling the wires in my push-up bra."

Finally satisfied that Mary wasn't a threat to national security, she directed her to the conveyor belt.

A TSA guy pointed to a leather object that could have doubled as a duffel bag. "Is this your purse, ma'am?"

"Yeah. Why?"

"We're going to have to take a look inside."

Mary looked at me, and I just shrugged my shoulders.

The poor inspector started unloading Mary's purse.

I doubt that Fibber McGee's closet held as much crap.

He held up a big bottle of Jergen's lotion. "Sorry, ma'am, you can't take this on the plane."

"But I have dry skin. Do you want me to itch all the way to Hawaii?"

Then he held up a metal flask. "What's in here, ma'am?"

"That's my medicine."

"What is it for?"

"It keeps me calm."

He unscrewed the lid and took a sniff. "Smells a lot like vodka."

"Yeah, but it sure keeps me calm."

He just looked at Mary and shook his head. By the time he was finished, Mary's purse didn't weigh as much.

It was still about forty-five minutes before boarding, so we found seats and busied ourselves reading, all except Willie who stared transfixed at the planes landing and taking off. I wondered if it was any comfort that none of them had crashed so far.

My attention was diverted from my reading by the emergence of another security guy being led by a huge German shepherd on a leash.

The dog went from bag to bag sniffing each one for explosives or drugs or other contraband. He was totally focused on the carry-on bags and seemed oblivious to the people around him until he came to me. After sniffing my bag, he poked his big nose between my legs and snorted.

What is it with big dogs and my crotch?

Finally, it was time to board.

The desk girl started barking boarding orders, and we dutifully queued up in our designated lines. Just as we were about to surrender our boarding passes, another TSA guy approached me.

"Sir, has anyone put anything in your luggage without your knowledge?"

I just stood there for a minute thinking about his question.

"If it was without my knowledge, how would I know?"

He was still thinking that one over as I backed slowly away and boarded my flight.

I had booked the seats with Maggie and me sitting across the aisle from Willie and Mary.

I whispered to Maggie, "Maybe I should sit with Willie this first time. He's kind of freaked out."

She agreed, and we swapped seats.

The huge jet engines roared to life, and the flight attendants warned us of all the terrible things that could happen. The plane backed away from the jet way and began to taxi down the runway. There was a brief pause, and the plane shuddered as the pilot goosed the engines for takeoff.

I had briefed Willie about the barf bag, and he clutched it tightly in his hand.

The big jet sprang forward and picked up speed as it raced down the runway.

I looked at Willie. If there is such a thing as a black man being white as a ghost, he was it. His eyes were as big as saucers, and just as the plane lifted off the ground, he grabbed my arm and squeezed. It was all I could do not to scream. I was sure it would leave a mark.

Finally, the plane leveled off, and Willie released the death grip on my arm.

Presently, the captain spoke over the intercom. "We have reached our cruising altitude of thirty-two thousand feet. It should be a smooth ride to Dallas. The temperature in Dallas is seventy-nine degrees with partly sunny skies. Enjoy your flight."

Willie whispered in my ear, "How much is thirty-two thousand feet?"

"That's about six miles."

"Up in de air?"

"Uh, yeah."

Willie just closed his eyes, and I think he was muttering a prayer.

The flight attendant announced that beverages were to be served. When the cart reached Mary's aisle, she ordered a diet coke. The attendant was about to move on when Mary asked, "What about nuts? Don't I get a bag of nuts?"

"No, ma'am, we don't serve nuts anymore."

"Okay then, how about some pretzels?"

"I'm sorry, ma'am. Kansas City to Dallas is a short flight, and we only serve beverages."

"Well damn!"

Yes, Mary, flying ain't what it used to be.

About a half hour into our flight, Mary leaned over the aisle. "Walt, which way to the can?"

I pointed the way, and Mary shuffled down the aisle.

About ten minutes passed, and I heard a loud buzzer at the rear of the plane. A man jumped from his seat and headed toward the lavatory. I looked back just in time to see Mary backed up against the wall with the man in her face.

This couldn't be good.

I unbuckled and made my way back just in time to hear Mary declare, "I was not smoking."

I tapped the man on the shoulder, and Air Marshal Grant turned to face me.

"You again!" He looked at Mary. "I suppose this is one of yours."

"Yes, Mary is with me. What in the world did she do?"

"She set off the smoke detectors in the lavatory. I thought the flight attendant made it clear that this is a nonsmoking flight."

"I already told you I don't smoke."

"Then what set off the smoke detectors?"

Mary looked sheepishly around. Of course every eye on the plane was on her.

"It's kind of personal."

"Please elaborate," Grant said.

"Well, if you must know, I took a dump. When I was done, it was awful ripe in there, so I just lit a match, you know, to get rid of the smell. I knew there was people waiting to come in after me. It was the polite thing to do."

Grant just rolled his eyes.

"Here," he said. "She's all yours. Now you owe me two."

I thanked him, and as I herded Mary down the aisle, I heard her mutter, "He probably thinks his shit don't stink."

Three weeks to go and this is just the first day. What have I done?

$$\text{⚖}$$

We had an hour layover in Dallas before boarding our flight to Honolulu. We grabbed a bite to eat and bought sandwiches and chips to eat on the flight.

We were waiting at the gate when Willie tugged on my arm.

"Mr. Walt, is all dees people going on de same plane as us?"

"Yes, I would say so."

"Cool."

Without hesitation, he made his way across the room and sat down by a lovely brown-skinned lady in her mid-fifties.

I had never really seen Willie in action. Stories of his legendary exploits were all secondhand but, as I soon learned, were not exaggerated.

I wished that I were close enough to hear because whatever he said caused the woman's face to light up, and soon the two were thoroughly engrossed in conversation. They talked until boarding was announced. He patted her arm, and as he grabbed his carry-on, he gave me a wink.

I noted that Willie's newfound friend was seated a few rows back from us, and as he moved down the aisle, I noticed a swagger that was certainly not present on the first leg of our flight. He gave her a big grin as he stowed his carry-on.

Willie, the cowardly flyer, had turned into Mr. Cool Dude, the veteran traveler.

Then I remembered a scene from the movie *48 Hours* where Eddie Murphy says to Nick Nolte, "Lack of pussy make you brave, man!"

Sometimes life imitates art.

It was a long six-and-a-half-hour flight from Dallas to Honolulu.

I noticed that there were several Hawaiians on the plane, which was not surprising. Buddy Kalakoa had told me that there were more Hawaiians living on the mainland than in the islands. Housing prices had risen to such heights that only the wealthy from the mainland, Canada, and Asia could afford to buy.

It was about three hours into the flight. The beverage cart had made its rounds, overpriced sandwiches had been sold, and the in-flight movie was playing on the screen.

Everyone had zoned out in his or her own way. Some were reading; others were sleeping or watching the movie.

Willie excused himself and headed to the lavatory at the rear of the aircraft. Shortly after, his lady friend headed in the same direction.

Oh boy!

It doesn't take a guy that long to take a leak, so when Willie didn't return right away, I read between the lines.

I heard the lavatory door close and saw the woman return to her seat. Willie discreetly stayed behind.

About that time, a large Hawaiian guy stood and made his way forward into the first class section. I knew this was a no-no and wondered what the guy was up to.

I soon found out.

I heard a scuffle and a scream, and he emerged back into the coach section with a flight attendant in his grip. The sharp end of a ballpoint pen was pressed against the carotid artery in her neck.

"No one move," he ordered, "or she will die."

He was backing down the aisle, and I saw Grant moving toward him from the first class section.

"Don't come any closer."

"Look, I'm a federal air marshal," Grant said. "Don't hurt anyone. What is it that you want?"

"You can contact the authorities on the mainland?"

"Yes."

"Four of my brothers were arrested in Kansas City. They are to be released or this woman will die."

Unbelievable! What were the chances that after all these weeks, we would book our flight on the same plane as the guys who wanted to roast us?

"You know we can't negotiate with terrorists."

"Terrorist! Is that what you called Washington and Jefferson when they fought to free the colonies from England? No! You called them patriots. I am a patriot, and I fight to free my people."

A Hawaiian man seated a few rows away spoke, "Bruddah, this is not the way to go. You are not helping our people. You are hurting our cause."

"*Auwe*, you say that because you have sold out to the *haoles*. We have waited for two hundred years for that which is rightfully ours to be returned. It is time for action."

"Hurting innocent people will not further our cause."

"In any revolution, there are those who will die. Sacrifices must be made. The old must be pruned away before the new can grow. Now go call the authorities. I have turned on my cell phone. When I receive a call from my brothers that they are safe, I will release the woman. Then you may do with me what you will."

He started backing toward the rear of the aircraft.

I had noticed that Willie had just started to return to his seat when the trouble started. He had ducked back into the lavatory and pulled the door closed.

Just as the huge Hawaiian came even with the lavatory, Willie kicked the door with all his might, and the door swung open, striking the Hawaiian in the back of the head.

Dazed, he released the flight attendant and slumped to the floor.

Grant was on him in an instant and cuffed his hands behind his back.

As I helped him move the helpless man to a sitting position, he leaned over and whispered in my ear, "Okay, now we're even."

After order had been restored, Willie returned to his seat.

He leaned over and asked, "Are we still flyin' at thirty-two thousand feet?"

"Yes, I suppose we are."

"Great! Den I'se a member of the Six Mile High Club."

Bragging rights. I was sure Louie the Lip would be impressed.

CHAPTER TEN

T he minute we stepped off the plane, we knew we were in a different world.

The fragrance of thousands of flower blossoms mingled with salt sea air, warmed by a tropical sun and delivered to us by gentle trade winds, assaulted our senses. The four of us just stood there breathing in the delicious elixir.

Eventually, we got in line with our fellow passengers and headed to the baggage claim area.

As we approached the crowded carousel, I saw a young man and woman holding a placard that said, "Williams party."

I waived and said, "I'm Walter Williams."

"Aloha, and welcome to the island. I am Jimmy, and this is my wife, Leilani. I am a cousin of Buddy Kalakoa and will be your guide while you are on Oahu."

Leilani stepped forward and placed a gorgeous white flower lei around my neck and kissed me on the cheek.

Then Jimmy's attention was directed to Maggie. "And you must be Hualani. Welcome, sister." He placed the same lei around her neck.

Evidently Buddy had shared Maggie's heritage with the family back home.

I thought Maggie was going to have an orgasm right there in the airport.

"What are these flowers? I've never smelled anything so wonderful in my whole life."

"This lei is made from the tuberose. It's wonderful fragrance is befitting one as lovely as you."

That Jimmy was really smooth. I'll bet he had done this before.

After Willie and Mary received their traditional Hawaiian greeting, we retrieved our bags and headed to Jimmy's van.

Our goal was to spend a few days on Oahu to get over the jet lag and see some sights before we flew to Kauai for the wedding.

It was almost seven in the evening when Jimmy dropped us off at our hotel. We had been in traveling mode for seventeen hours, and we were all exhausted.

"You guys get some supper and a good night's rest, and I'll pick you up at nine thirty in the morning."

Our hotel was the Sheraton Waikiki, right on the water at the north end of the famous Waikiki Beach.

We decided to just get some sandwiches to take to our rooms and chill out for the evening.

Our room was on the twenty-fifth floor. We stowed our bags, threw open the drapes, and stepped onto the lanai. I'll never forget the sight that met our eyes.

Our room faced the west, and the sun was just beginning to slide into the azure blue water of the Pacific. The puffy clouds above were painted with a hundred different hues of red and gold. The gentle waves washed onto the shores of Waikiki Beach, and in the distance Diamond Head reflected the last dazzling rays of the setting sun.

We held each other close and just stood there until the last remnants of daylight surrendered to the night.

Then an entirely different but just as beautiful scene unfolded.

In the distance we could see the red and green running lights of passing ships, and Waikiki Beach came alive with thousands of twinkling lights as far as we could see. It looked as if a fairy had scattered her glittering dust along the beach.

Just when we were about to call it a day, a strange glow arose from behind Diamond Head. We stood in awe as a full moon slowly raised its head from behind the enormous crater. As it rose in the sky, its beams cast silvery, undulating shadows on the ocean swells.

Maggie gave me a squeeze. "Walt, it's just perfect. I can't tell you how much this means to me."

"Me too. You know, this is our first night in paradise. I can only think of one thing that could make it more perfect. What do you think?"

"I think I need to take a shower and freshen up. Then let's see what develops."

"Sounds good to me."

Maggie hit the bathroom first and stood under the hot shower so long I began to wonder if there would be any hot water left for me.

She finally emerged, wrapped in a fluffy towel.

"Okay, big boy. Your turn, and I'll be right here waiting for you." She patted the bed.

When the hot spray from the shower hit my body, I realized why she had dawdled so long. It felt great. I stood there until I started to get pink and wrinkly.

I dried, wrapped a towel around my rosy body, and headed to the bedroom with visions of ecstasy dancing in my head.

And there was my beautiful bride-to-be—sound asleep.

Paradise would have to wait.

I was asleep as soon as my head hit the pillow.

I slept soundly until I felt Maggie thrashing around. I looked at my watch. It was three thirty in the morning.

I rolled over and tried to close my eyes, but they just wouldn't cooperate. I was wide-awake.

Then I heard Maggie whisper, "Are you awake?"

"Yep."

"But it's the middle of the night."

"Not to our bodies. They think its eight thirty."

"So this is jet lag, huh?"

"As long as we're up, how about a walk along the beach? It probably won't be real crowded."

"Sounds good to me."

We slipped on our swimsuits and flip-flops and headed to the beach.

The moon was starting its descent into the horizon but was still high enough into the sky to illuminate the waves as they broke along the beach.

We strolled hand in hand, letting the surf wrap around our feet and ankles. Each time the tide came in, Maggie would squeal and giggle and dance, and it made me love her even more.

In the distance, I saw something bobbing up and down in the surf. I had read about the tide washing flotsam and jetsam ashore, and I assumed it was a bag of trash or a Styrofoam cooler that had fallen off a passing ship.

As we drew near, the bobbing object suddenly sprouted arms and a head and began frantically waving.

It was Mary.

"Hey, Mr. Walt. Come on in. The water's great."

"Uh, thanks. I think we'll pass."

"Okay, then I'll come in."

As she emerged from the deep, the first image that popped into my mind was from the 1954 movie classic *The Creature From The Black Lagoon* as the monster silently slipped from the water.

Only this time, it was my old friend wearing nothing but an itsy bitsy, teeny weenie, yellow polka dot bikini.

No matter how dear the friend, there are just some things that shouldn't be seen.

I didn't know they even made bikinis that size.

I whispered to Maggie, "That is just wrong on so many levels."

She whispered back, "Try not to look."

I averted my eyes and saw Willie sitting in the sand. I hadn't noticed him before. He sort of blended into the background, it being night and all.

I gave him a quizzical look, and he just shrugged his shoulders.

There are just some things you can't control.

Willie and Mary joined us for the remainder of our beach walk. I found comfort in the fact that no one else was awake to see this odd foursome strolling Waikiki Beach.

It probably wouldn't be good for tourism.

We returned to the Sheraton just at daybreak, showered, dressed, and reconvened in the hotel dining room.

The breakfast buffet was what you dream about.

As I surveyed the sumptuous array and the beautiful setting, the words of a song from *South Pacific* came to mind:

> We've got sunlight on the sand; we've got moonlight on the sea.
>
> We've got mangos and bananas you can pick right off the tree.

Sure enough, there were mangos, bananas, papaya, pineapple, carved ham, omelets, basically anything to please the tourist palate.

I think I gained three pounds just looking at it.

We finished our lavish breakfast just in time to meet Jimmy in front of the hotel.

"Climb in. I've got a great day planned for us on the south side of the island. First stop, Hanauma Bay."

Jimmy was a great guide. The Hanauma Bay Nature Reserve was magnificent, and we were blessed to have someone along who had grown up on the island. He shared his personal insights and stories, which made the experience even more memorable.

The next stop was Sea Life Park. This attraction was obviously designed with the tourist in mind. There were shows featuring birds, turtles, penguins, and, of course, the bottle-nosed dolphin.

Jimmy led us into a large covered arena with stadium seats circling a large pool. He directed us to some seats high above the pool.

Mary took exception.

"This is the dolphin show, right? I love dolphins, so I ain't gonna sit way up there. I want to be right here by the glass where I can see them up close and personal."

Jimmy just shrugged. He already figured out that there was no point in arguing with Mary.

The dolphins were wonderful. They jumped, waved their fins, balanced balls, and did all kinds of fabulous tricks. I could see that Mary was having a ball.

At the conclusion of the show, the MC announced that anyone sitting up close might want to move back a few rows.

Not Mary. You know, up close and personal.

The dolphins swam in circles around the pool, gaining speed with each lap. Finally, the trainer gave the signal, and all three dolphins came out of the water and crashed down in a thundering back flip that sent a tidal wave cascading over the edge of the pool—right on top of Mary.

The crowd roared, the dolphins grinned, and all I heard out of Mary was, "Well, damn!"

The sign next to her seat reading "splash zone" probably took on new meaning for her.

Sea Life Park is right on the ocean, and there are wild birds everywhere. "Wild" might be somewhat of a misnomer. While these birds certainly weren't in captivity, they had lived around people all their lives and were not intimidated by our presence.

Quite the contrary, they knew we humans were good for a handout, and our feathered friends, from tiny sparrows to seagulls with eighteen-inch wingspans, followed us around hoping for a tasty morsel.

Like much of the US citizenry, they had discovered it was much easier to live on the dole than to actually work for their food.

Park officials discouraged such behavior and had posted signs everywhere admonishing us, "Please don't feed the birds."

It was a futile effort. Either all the tourists are illiterate or just don't give a damn. There was plenty for the birds to eat.

We were getting hungry too, so we headed to the snack bar and ordered burgers and fries, traditional Hawaiian fare.

We found a table in the shade of a beautiful plumeria tree in full blossom. It was so relaxing, just sitting in this beautiful place with friends—friends feeding the birds!

Mary was pinching off little bits of her French fries and coaxing a little brown dove closer and closer to the table.

I was about to admonish her when I heard Willie exclaim, "Hey, I didn't want no mayonnaise on my sandwich."

I looked at Willie's sandwich, and I looked in the tree directly over his head.

A big white gull peered back at us, and I swear he was smiling.

"Uh, Willie, I wouldn't eat that if I were you."

Willie looked up and, like Mary, simply muttered, "Well, damn!"

We were back at the Sheraton by late afternoon. Jimmy told us to shower and relax, and he would pick us up at seven for dinner.

It wasn't far down the strip to Duke's Barefoot Bar on the Beach. The restaurant was named after Duke Kahanamoku, the famous Hawaiian surfer. The atmosphere was exactly what we had hoped for: soft Hawaiian music, the surf and sand a stone's throw away, good food, and fruity drinks with little umbrellas.

Mary was in hog heaven.

As she proudly hoisted her first piña colada, it brought to mind Steve Martin in *The Jerk* as he jauntily lifted his umbrella drink and proclaimed, "Be somebody!"

The restaurant was packed, and I noticed many of the diners wore little badges. We were obviously in the midst of a convention crowd.

While this wasn't exactly a Hooters restaurant, it was obvious that the waitresses weren't hired for their serving skills alone. Island beauties with long black hair, dressed in short, formfitting sheaths, scurried among the diners delivering food and drinks.

The booze flowed freely, and after enough mai tais to float a battleship, the convention boys started acting like sailors on shore leave.

I had noticed one particularly obnoxious guy trying to cop a feel. The waitress had deftly sidestepped the intended grope and moved on without causing a scene. But when the next round was delivered, he had apparently decided not to take no for an answer.

While both her hands were busy balancing a tray of drinks, Mr. Macho grabbed a handful of tush and squeezed.

"Please, sir. Don't do that," she said.

"Aw, come on, honey. You know you like it. Besides, if you're not asking for it, how come you're dressing that way?" And with that, he slipped his arms around her waist and grabbed a cheek with each hand.

"Please! Stop!" she pleaded.

I had seen enough.

I normally try not to get involved in other people's affairs, but macho bullies abusing women is one of my hot buttons.

Without really giving much thought to the consequences, I rose from my seat and approached the offending oaf.

"Look, mister, the lady asked you nicely to let go. Why not give her a break?"

He just looked at me in disbelief. "Butt out, grandpa."

"Sorry, I can't do that."

He was obviously not used to being talked back to, and I soon discovered why.

He released the girl, and as he lifted his six-foot-two, 220 pound frame out of the chair, I noticed his nametag that read, "Earl, Building Contractor's Convention."

Oops!

I could tell right away that he was really pissed. The fire in his eyes told me I was in trouble, but the booze in his belly leveled the playing field.

He reared back to deliver a roundhouse you could see coming from a mile away. The alcohol dulled his reflexes just enough for me to duck under the huge fist, which landed squarely on the chin of a busboy who was unfortunate enough to be passing by. The tray flew into the air and landed in the middle of the table, spewing leftovers into the laps of Earl's dining companions. They leaped from their seats and converged on me like a pack of hyenas on a gazelle.

The first guy to reach me was about to exact his revenge, when a black streak hit him from behind and took him to the floor.

If I didn't know better, I would have sworn that Willie had been a linebacker for the Kansas City Chiefs.

In the meantime, the busboys had come to the rescue of their fallen comrade. It was obvious that the boozed-up conventioneers were no match for these sleek island guys.

I was just picking myself up when I noticed out of the corner of my eye that Earl was swinging a tray at the back of my head. The last thing I heard before the lights went out was sirens wailing in the distance.

When I regained consciousness, I found my head resting in Willie's lap.

Slowly, I rose up, my head nearly exploding. When my senses finally returned, I looked around and found myself—in jail?

I looked at Willie.

He just grinned and said, "I guess we done took care of those guys, didn't we?" Then he pointed to the cell across the room.

Earl and his cohorts were slumped on the floor nursing cuts, bruises, and the mother of all hangovers.

I had never been on this side of the bars before, and it was a strange feeling. As I sat contemplating our situation, the words Elvis sang in a similar situation in *Blue Hawaii* came to mind:

> I'm a poor Hawaiian beach boy, a long way from the beach, 'cause someone shoved his face against my hand.
>
> Now I'm a kissing cousin to a ripe pineapple; I'm in the can.

I heard a commotion in the hallway and saw a smiling Jimmy coming down the hall with a guard.

"Well, bro, you sure earned your Hawaiian name last night: Kamamalu, the protector. You're kind of a hero."

"How come I don't feel like a hero? And what's my captain going to say when he finds out I'm in jail?"

"You aren't in jail anymore. My cousin manages Dukes, and he told the cops how you rescued Maile from those creeps. You're free to go."

The guard unlocked the door, and we followed Jimmy to his waiting van. Maggie was waiting for me inside, and I was hoping for a hero's welcome.

It was then I noticed that I was covered in blood, garbage, puke, and stale booze.

Maggie rolled her eyes, covered her nose, and moved to the front seat beside Jimmy.

My hero's welcome would have to wait.

The next two days were terrific.

Jimmy took us across the Pali to the Polynesian Cultural Center on the other side of the island, and we visited beautiful Waimea Falls Park on the north shore. We did all of the wonderful things that every tourist does that makes Hawaii one of the best vacation spots on the planet.

We had one day left on Oahu, and Jimmy asked if there was anything else we wanted to see.

"Jimmy, you've been a wonderful guide and friend, and we have loved all the places you have taken us, but so far everything has been the usual tourist places. I know this stuff is all commercial. It's not the real Hawaii. I want you to take us to the village near Waimanolo."

His back stiffened. "Why in the world would you want to go there? That's no place for *haoles*."

"Jimmy, I know that Buddy has told you about our involvement with the stolen artifacts and the murders of his grandfather and uncle. And don't forget people associated with that village kidnapped Maggie and me. I have learned a lot about the history of your people, and I want to see the real Hawaii, firsthand."

"I am a modern boy, but I also know you should not tempt the old ones. Do you remember the old Jim Croce song that says, 'You don't tug on Superman's cape; you don't spit into the wind; you don't pull the mask off the old Lone Ranger,' and in this case you don't mess around with things you don't understand."

"Uncle Ray told us that the islands would call us and that we had been chosen. I don't think he meant just to go to Pearl Harbor. Something is definitely going on that we don't understand, but I think we're a part of it, whether we like it or not. Now are you going to take us to Waimanolo, or do I have to rent a car?"

Reluctantly he agreed. We decided it might be prudent to leave Willie and Mary by the pool.

It was a beautiful drive around the south tip of the island.

When we reached Waimanolo, it looked, on the surface, like any of the other small towns on the island. There were hotels, restaurants, and places wanting you to get married on Waimanolo Beach.

"So what's so different here?" I asked, somewhat disappointed. I wasn't sure if I was expecting guys in loincloths and women in ti leaf skirts living in grass shacks on the beach.

"On the surface, nothing," he replied. "But let's take a little drive into the Koolau Mountains."

We left the city, and housing tracts turned into rural cottages. Every few miles a sign was posted that read, "*Kapu.*"

"Did Buddy tell you what that means?" Jimmy asked.

"I believe the translation is 'forbidden' and was part of the early Hawaiians' social structure."

"Very good. But today it also means, 'Keep out,' as in 'You are forbidden to come on my property.'"

Interspersed with the *kapu* signs were other signs admonishing us to "Go home!"

I was beginning to get the picture.

We came to a wide spot in the road where a local farmer had set up a fruit and vegetable stand.

Jimmy pulled over, and we hopped out to get a better look at the local flavor—and did we ever!

One huge Hawaiian guy wore a T-shirt that read, "If it's called tourist season, why can't we shoot them?"

Whoa!

His buddy, equally large, wore a T-shirt depicting a white guy in a tub of boiling water surrounded by hungry-looking Hawaiians, with the inscription, "*Haole*—the other white meat."

I looked at Jimmy. He just rolled his eyes and shrugged as if to say, "I told you so."

I was about to grab Maggie by the arm and hurry her back to the car, but when we turned, a large, old, weather-worn woman blocked our path.

She leaned forward and whispered, "We know who you are."

It was a quiet ride back to Honolulu.

CHAPTER ELEVEN

We were in the process of packing our bags for the island hop from Oahu to Kauai when I noticed the headline in the *Honolulu Star Bulletin*.

It read, "Artifacts Slated for Permanent Display in Bishop Museum Hijacked."

I dropped what I was doing and dialed Buddy Kalakoa.

"Buddy here."

"Hi, Buddy. This is Walt. What in the world is going on?"

"Guess you saw the morning paper, huh?"

"Sure did. I thought the artifacts were traveling under guard. What happened?"

"The container carrying the artifacts was on a barge being towed to the harbor by a tug boat. Sometime during the night, thieves boarded the barge, broke into the container, and removed the artifacts."

"But where was the guard?"

"He was on the tug. Sometimes there is as much as a quarter mile of cable separating the tug from the barge. Those things don't have brakes, you know. Under the cover of darkness, the thieves must have pulled a small craft behind the barge, effectively blocking the guard's view, and emptied the container."

"How did they know which container carried the artifacts? I've seen those barges. There may be twenty or more containers on one load."

"Your guess is as good as mine, but somehow they knew. It was the only container that was opened."

"Kind of has the earmarks of an inside job, don't you think?"

"That was our thought. We handpicked everyone who was associated with the exhibit, but in this day and age, sometimes you just don't know where people's sympathies lie."

"So you think the separatists are responsible?"

"That's our best guess."

"If that's true, what will they do with the artifacts?"

"They have maintained from the beginning that the artifacts should never have been removed from the burial cave. They believe that their removal has angered Pele and the only way to regain her favor is to return the artifacts to their resting place and offer sacrifices to appease the transgression."

"Uh, sacrifices?"

"In the old days, to break a *kapu* meant instant death. If even the shadow of a commoner fell upon an *alii*, he was killed. The *kapu* was everything. My grandfather and uncle died by fire and the ceremonial war club to atone for their transgressions."

"What about you? Won't they hold you to blame as well?"

"Of course that's a possibility, but I feel an obligation to finish what my family has started. Some things are greater than the individual. I must see this through."

"So you think there may be more sacrifices?"

"Pele has great *mana*. It will take more than the deaths of two old fools to appease her. The blood of an *alii* must be spilled before she will rest."

That's not what I wanted to hear.

The flight from Honolulu to Kauai takes only about twenty minutes, and we were soon in the concourse of the Lihue airport.

I looked around for another "Williams Party" placard and found it in the hands of a twenty-something Hawaiian guy.

I waved, and he approached.

"Hi, I'm Walt Williams. And don't tell me, you're a cousin to Buddy Kalakoa."

"Yeah, bro, on my mother's side."

I had learned that much like our small rural towns in Missouri, everyone in Hawaii seemed to be related to everyone else, either by blood or marriage.

"My name is Sammy, and I'm also a nephew of Uncle Larry. I'll be taking care of you until your wedding, day after tomorrow."

Day after tomorrow!

I looked at Maggie and saw the shock in her eyes as well. We had been so absorbed in our vacation that the wedding had kind of sneaked up on us.

"Let's get you to your hotel. Unpack, get a bite of lunch, and this afternoon we'll take a trip to the fern grotto."

The Marriott Resort in Lihue was nothing like the Sheraton. The monolithic skyscraper on Oahu occupied very little ground space; by contrast, the Marriott covered acres of ground right on the water. The road into the resort, lined with stately palms on each side, was just a harbinger of the elegance that awaited us inside. There were lush garden pools with brightly colored birds and fish, and the halls were lined with sculpture and Hawaiian art.

And that was just the lobby.

We registered and walked to the terrace overlooking the interior grounds.

Wow!

The largest swimming pool I had ever seen was surrounded by lounges, massage tables, waterfalls, spas, and restaurants. We stood in awe as we took in the pool and the beach and ocean beyond.

For once in her life, Mary was at a loss for words.

I thought I heard Willie mumble, "Sumbitch!"

If this is how the other half lives, I could sure get used to it.

Well, maybe not.

We unpacked and ate lunch in the restaurant by the pool. We were all reluctant to leave, but we had promised Sammy that we would be by the bell desk at one o'clock.

It was a relatively short drive from Lihue north to Kapa'a and the Waimea River.

Kauai was nothing like Honolulu with its freeways and sprawling city. Everything seemed more rural and small town.

We pulled into the parking lot on the south side of the river, and Sammy pointed to the other shore.

"That's the Coco Palms over there. That's where you will be getting married."

I looked expectantly in the direction he had pointed, and I'm sure my mouth must have fallen open.

I don't know what I was expecting, but it certainly wasn't that.

A high wall surrounded what had once been the resort, and a sign on a locked gate warned, "No admittance! Authorized personnel only!"

Looking beyond the gate, I could see nothing but the tops of palms that had been ravaged by the hurricane and a few ramshackle huts that had been left to deteriorate.

Maggie's reaction was the same as mine. I could see in her eyes that she was not excited about celebrating the most important day of her life in a ghost town.

Sammy must have seen the look on our faces.

"Hey, bro, not to worry. You're gonna love it. Uncle Larry has been doing this for years, and nobody's been unhappy yet."

I hoped he was right.

The trip up the Waimea River was unremarkable. We learned cool stuff, such as Kauai is the northernmost of the islands and therefore geologically the oldest. It is the only island with a river, and the river is fed from Mount Wai'ale'ale, the wettest spot on earth, averaging over four hundred and sixty inches of rain a year.

I made mental notes because stuff like that really impresses people at parties.

The grotto itself was beautiful, but for me it turned out to be one of those been-there-done-that kind of things.

There were two old Hawaiian guys on board whose job was to serenade us with island favorites to take our minds off how bored we were as the barge chugged up and down the river.

The thing that saved the afternoon for me was when Sammy told me that one of the old guys, as a young boy, was an extra in the filming of *Blue Hawaii* and knew Elvis.

I became totally engrossed in his tales of the "old days," when the Coco Palms was the premier resort in the islands and how Hawaii came to have a special place in the heart of the King.

Before I knew it, we were back at the dock. This chance meeting had made the whole trip worthwhile.

Sammy took us back to the Marriott and before driving off promised us that we would be thrilled with our trip to Waimea Canyon, the Grand Canyon of the Pacific, scheduled for the next day.

It turns out that good old Duke had another restaurant within walking distance of the hotel, so we agreed to freshen up, meet by the pool, and enjoy a leisurely stroll to dinner.

I showered first and had just buttoned my new aloha shirt when the phone rang.

"Hello? This is Walt."

"Hi, son. We've got a problem."

"Dad! What kind of a problem?"

"Well, the contractor—"

Just then there was a knock at the door.

"Hang on, Dad. Someone's at the door. I'll be right back."

I opened the door, and two very serious-looking Hawaiian policemen stepped into the room.

"Are you Walter Williams?"

"Yes, I am. What can I do for you?"

One of them handed me a cell phone. "This is for you."

I had no idea what was going on, but I took the phone. "This is Walt Williams. Who's this?"

I couldn't believe what I heard next.

"Walt, this is Captain Short. I'm afraid I have some bad news."

Immediately, the thought that crossed my mind was that someone close to me was hurt or dead.

"What . . . what's wrong? Is someone hurt?"

"No, nothing like that. I almost wish it were that simple. Walt, there's a warrant for your arrest. You're wanted for murder."

I was speechless.

"Walt, I need you to come home and clear this up."

"But I'm getting married day after tomorrow," I stammered.

"I know that and I'm sorry. If you won't come back voluntarily—that is, if you want to stay and get married—it will take a few days to get extradition papers to Hawaii. I just figured you wouldn't want to get married with this thing hanging over your head."

"No, of course not. But what's this all about? Who was I supposed to have killed?"

"I can't really talk about that right now. Am I to understand that you are willing to come home without extradition?"

"Well, there's no point in getting married if I'm going to be dragged away from my honeymoon."

"I thought you would probably say that, so I have sent an officer to accompany you back to Kansas City. I'm afraid you'll be under arrest until we get this straightened out. I'm so sorry, Walt."

I handed the phone back to the officer.

The two Hawaiian guys stepped aside, and a man in a Kansas City police uniform stepped into the room.

Murdock!

Of all the officers in the Kansas City police department, Murdock was the last guy I wanted to see.

For some reason that escapes me to this day, Murdock hates my guts.

He was on my case from my first day on the force and has gone out of his way to give me grief and disparage the City Retiree Action Patrol.

The fact that I was responsible for the arrest of his friend and mentor, Captain Harrington, had only made it worse.

There was no love lost between us.

I could see the hate in his eyes as he held up the handcuffs. "Walter Williams, you are under arrest for murder. Now turn around and put your hands behind your back."

"Cuffs? Is that really necessary? I'm coming voluntarily."

"Shut up, old man, and turn around."

Murdock was reading me my rights when Maggie stepped into the room wrapped in a towel.

"Walt—what?"

"I have no idea what's going on. Call Ozzie Meacham, and tell him to find out where this creep is taking me and to meet me there. This must be some kind of a horrible mistake. I'll call you as soon as I know something."

"I'm coming with you."

"No, you can't leave Willie and Mary here alone. Let Sammy know that the wedding is on hold until we get this straightened out."

The last thing I heard as Murdock led me away was Dad's voice booming through the receiver, "Walt! Walt! What the hell's going on over there?"

I wish I knew.

CHAPTER TWELVE

The red-eye from Honolulu back to Kansas City wasn't nearly as much fun as the trip over.

If you think sitting in one of those cramped seats for eight hours is tough under normal circumstances, try doing it in handcuffs.

The lavatory was another nightmare.

My experience on previous flights was that I seemed to time my stream just as the plane hit an air pocket. After a few episodes of misdirection, I learned to steady myself using one hand on the wall and the other for guidance.

You can't do that with your wrists shackled together.

I suspect that the lady who came in after me wasn't too thrilled.

I tried to question Murdock as to the details of my incarceration, but he refused to discuss anything about the case. He said his job was to simply bring me in.

From the airport, I was taken directly to the precinct and placed in a holding room. As I stared at the four blank walls, I reflected on how my life had so abruptly changed. In just over a week, I had gone from celebrated head of the City Retiree Action Patrol to common criminal with two arrests a half a world apart.

I had just started my pity party when I heard a knock, and Captain Short and Ozzie Meacham entered the room.

Fortunately, I have had very few occasions in my life to use the services of an attorney.

Ozzie Meacham was the attorney on retainer for my former employer, City Wide Realty. In my thirty years there, I had come to know Ozzie and had taken his counsel on a couple of particularly sticky real estate deals.

I was relieved to see them both. "Would someone please tell me what's going on?"

Ozzie spoke first. "Before we get into that, I know that you and Captain Short are friends, but this is different. You're on opposite sides of the fence, and you might want to think about talking with me privately."

I looked at Shorty. "Nope, I've got nothing to hide. I know I can trust the captain, and he will do whatever he can to help me. Now will somebody *please* tell me why I'm locked up?"

"It's your building," the captain said. "You hired a contractor to remodel while you were away. He was tearing down walls between your two units, and they found a body enclosed between the studs."

"A *body?*"

"Well, actually a skeleton, or at least most of a skeleton. They're still poking around trying to find all the pieces."

"And you think I put it there?"

"Of course I don't, Walt, but there is a lot of evidence pointing in your direction."

"Such as?"

"How long have you owned the building?

"Going on thirty years. So what?"

"So these bones are old—really old. Possibly placed there during the early days of your ownership. If so, you would be the only person who could have known about the construction necessary to conceal the body."

"But I haven't done anything to the building other than carpet and paint."

"At this point, I guess it's just your word on that."

"And how do they know how old the bones are? What if they were put there before I bought the building? I thought they had tests for that stuff."

"They do, but that takes a while. In the meantime, you're all they've got."

"So I'm in jail, my wedding is canceled, and my life is a mess because a skeleton was found in a building I own? Is that all they've got?"

"Not exactly."

"Great! What else?"

"They found a Teamsters' Union pin with the body."

"So what's that got to do with me?"

"How long were you a realtor?"

"Thirty years. I bought the building my first year in the business."

"So that would have been around 1980?"

"Yeah, that's about right."

"What did you do the ten years before you were a real estate agent?"

"Let's see. I was in college, then I worked for the post office for four years, then... then I ran a route for Wonder Bread for two years."

"You drove a truck for Wonder Bread?"

"Oh crap! I see where this is going. I was in the Teamsters' Union for those two years. I had no choice.

If you wanted to drive, you had to be in the union. But I never even attended a meeting."

"But you can see how it all ties together."

"Ozzie, can you get me out of here?"

"Maybe. Everything they have is circumstantial. They are going to want to grill you, but after that I can get you out on bail."

Grill was certainly an appropriate term. After hours in which authorities looked under every rock in my life, I was released on bail with the admonition, "Don't leave town."

I called Maggie immediately. She had been out of her mind with worry. She had picked up the phone after my abrupt departure, and Dad had filled her in on what he knew.

After I gave her the gory details of my incarceration, I told her to hang tight and try to enjoy her vacation.

I also assured her that her betrothed was not an axe murderer.

It was not much comfort under the circumstances.

My next stop was the office of Stewart Title Insurance. I knew that I didn't bury the body, so it had to be someone who owned the building before me. I needed to run a chain of title.

I had given hundreds of transactions worth a bundle to Stewart Title over the years, so I figured they owed me a favor.

Ester Waterman had been my favorite title examiner over the years. She had closed many a transaction for both Maggie and me.

"Hi, Esther. How's the title business?"

"Walt! So good to see you. Business is so-so. I'm keeping busy."

"Not too busy to do me a favor, I hope."

"Just name it."

"I need you to run a chain of title, back to, say, 1960." I gave her the address.

"Isn't that your building?"

"Yep. You've got a good memory."

"I just hope our computer records go back that far. If not, it would be a real pain to have to dig it out by hand. That would take some time."

"Time isn't something I have in abundance right now, so good luck."

She poked around on the computer for a few minutes and finally announced, "You're in luck. We go back to 1955 on that property, and let's see. Looks there have only been three owners since that time. You bought the building in 1980 from Arnold Gobel, and he bought it in 1977 from Nicolas Civella. That's as far back as we go."

"Can you print that out for me?"

"Absolutely. Hey, wait a minute. Aren't you supposed to be in Hawaii marrying Maggie McBride?"

"It's a long story."

I thanked her and headed home to boot up the computer.

On the way home, my cell phone beeped.

"Walt, it's Ozzie. I have some news. I don't know how much help this will be, but the cops have released the information that the skeleton was not intact when they found it. It looks like the body was dismembered before it was enclosed behind the wall."

"Swell. I suppose now they will want to check out all my hand tools for body parts."

"Actually, I think they may have already done that."

"You're kidding me."

"No, I'm afraid you may find your apartment in kind of a mess. They're not real careful when they search a place."

When I arrived home, Dad and the professor were sitting on the porch. They wouldn't let me pass until I had brought them up to date on the investigation.

"Look, guys, I've got to get to my computer and look up the two previous owners of the building. This has got to be connected to one of them."

"What are their names?" Dad asked.

I opened the printout that Esther had given me. "Arnold Gobel and Nicholas Civella."

Dad and the professor exchanged knowing looks.

"What? Are these names supposed to mean something to me?"

"Well, I don't know about that Gobel fellow, but Nick Civella should ring a few bells."

"How so?"

"The Civella family, Nick and his brother, Carl, ran the Kansas City mob for years, starting in the early seventies."

"Well, that certainly could explain a lot of things."

Then the professor chimed in, "In addition to gambling, prostitution, and the usual mob stuff, they also operated legitimate businesses that they used to launder their illegal money."

"And don't forget the teamsters," Dad said. "They had Roy Lee Williams, the president, in their pocket and financed all kinds of things with loans from the teamsters' pension fund."

"I need to find out more about those guys. I'd better get to the computer."

"I think I can do better than that," the professor said. "My old friend from the university, Professor Winkle, studied crime in Kansas City extensively from the early Pendergast years clear through the debacle in the River Quay. He can tell you more than you will ever find on Google."

"Great! Hook me up."

Professor Winkle lived in the Brookside area in one of those stately Victorian homes covered with ivy and gingerbread molding.

"Professor Skinner filled me in on what you're looking for," he said as he led me into his library. "The Civella family has quite a history in Kansas City."

"Yes, evidently he used to own the building that I now own, and I'm wondering what other ties he had to local businesses."

"Let's take a look," he said as he opened a thick notebook. "In addition to several apartment buildings like yours—let's see—they also had ties to a trucking company, some bars and strip clubs, a construction company, and a medical waste disposal company."

"Well, the construction company could certainly be a tie-in. Do you have addresses for all of the places?"

"Certainly, but understand, this was forty years ago. Those businesses most likely don't even exist today."

After listening to an hour of Kansas City crime history, I thanked the professor and headed home. As I drove, I kept going over the ties to the Civella family.

There was something there that seemed to be tugging at me, but I couldn't quite put my finger on it.

Then it struck me.

Just before we had left for Hawaii, there had been a major story in the *Kansas City Star* about a local company that disposed of medical waste.

I had never really given it a thought before. What do they do with the stuff they take out of you at the hospital? Do they just put your old appendix down the garbage disposal?

And what about the folks that are organ donors? What happens to the leftovers?

Nowadays, the stuff is labeled "biohazard medical waste" and is shipped to facilities where it is incinerated.

The stink came when containers filled with body parts arrived in Kansas City, Kansas, and it turned out to be the remains of somebody's loved one who was supposed to have been cremated and sitting in an urn on the mantle.

Who was actually in the urn was anybody's guess.

Apparently huge quantities of body parts are constantly being shipped all over the United States for disposal.

Who keeps track of all this stuff?

If I were an underworld crime boss, I couldn't think of a better operation to own to get rid of the remains of some poor sap I just had whacked.

I parked and was headed for my apartment when Jerry collared me in the lobby.

"Hey, Walt. Your dad told me about your problems. Any breaks yet?"

Naturally I had to retell the whole story.

Jerry followed me upstairs. The doors were still sealed with crime scene tape, but I had been told that the authorities were through processing the scene.

I opened the door, and—*yikes!* I think "processing" may have been an understatement.

Every drawer and cabinet stood open, their contents strewn about. Chairs and the couch were overturned, and the bed was totally disassembled.

This, along with the construction debris, gave the appearance that Hurricane Iniki had made a curtain call. I realized my mistake immediately when I said as much out loud.

Jerry pounced on that one immediately. "Walt, do you know what one palm tree said to the other as the hurricane approached?"

"No, but I'm sure you're going to tell me."

"Hang on to your nuts; I think we're in for a big blow."

I just love being Dean Martin to his Jerry Lewis.

To Jerry's credit, he pitched in, and an hour later the place had been restored to some semblance of order.

I was about to boot up the computer when the phone rang.

"Walt, Captain Short here. I have some good news for you."

"Terrific. I could use some good news about now. Do you know what those goons did to my apartment?"

"Yeah, sorry about that, but maybe this will ease your pain. I pulled in some favors and got a rush on the carbon dating on the skeleton. While they can't pinpoint the exact time of death, it does appear that the body was sealed up prior to your ownership. Looks like you're off the hook."

"That is good news, but why couldn't they have done all that before they drug my sorry ass all the way back from Hawaii?"

"Yeah, that's a real bummer. Anyway, they're now going to take a hard look at the previous owners of the building. They now figure that the Teamsters' pin probably belonged to the victim rather than the killer."

"I think I can help with that. By the way, am I free to rejoin my lovely bride?"

"Absolutely. Go with our blessing."

I briefed the captain on my title search and meeting with Professor Winkle.

My first call was to Maggie. She was overjoyed with the news.

We still had three days left on Kauai before we were scheduled to fly to Maui. I told her to call Sammy and see if Uncle Larry was still available, and I would catch the first available flight back to the islands.

I called Dad, Jerry, and the professor together to share the good news.

After I brought them up to date on the status of the investigation, Jerry and the professor were all smiles and congratulations, but Dad just sat there deep in thought.

"What's up, Dad? What's on your mind?"

"So now they think the body was buried sometime prior to 1980 and that the victim was a teamster?"

"That's the way I understand it. Why is that important?"

"It's probably nothing. Naw, it just couldn't be."

"What couldn't be?" Now Dad had me curious.

"Well, I know of a teamster who disappeared in 1975, and his body was never found."

The professor bolted upright. "You don't think—no, it's just too incredible."

"But the timing is right," Dad said. "Sonny, didn't you say Civella owned the building until 1977?"

"Yes. Now what are you talking about? Who is this mystery victim?"

Dad and the professor said the name simultaneously.

"Jimmy Hoffa."

"What? No way."

"It's a stretch," the professor said, "but let's consider some facts. Hoffa was president of the teamsters until he was convicted of jury tampering in 1964. It was no secret that he was connected with the mob. When he went to jail, he selected Frank Fitzsimmons to lead the union.

"He served five years and was given a pardon by Nixon in 1971. He had to wait five more years before he could try to assume his old position as president of the union."

"Yeah," Dad said, "and he didn't waste any time. As soon as he was released, he started lining up support for his takeover. Unfortunately for him, the mob liked working with Fitzsimmons. Hoffa was a real hard ass and difficult to control. Fitzsimmons was easier to handle. It was a tough time for us rank and file members. Hoffa was one of those guys you either hated or loved. There was no middle ground."

"Hoffa disappeared on July thirtieth, nineteen seventy-five," the professor continued. "He was in

Bloomfield, Michigan, and was supposed to be meeting with some mob guys from Detroit. He was last seen in a car owned by Joe Giacalone, who ran the Detroit operation. Authorities found Hoffa's DNA in the car, but Giacalone had an airtight alibi."

"Everyone knew that the mob whacked him," Dad said, "but there was never any direct evidence, and his body has never been found."

I started putting the pieces of the puzzle together.

"So what you're saying is that the Detroit guys nabbed him, dismembered the body, and shipped it to Civella's medical waste facility here in Kansas City? Why didn't they just burn it along with the other medical waste?"

"Who knows about those mob guys. They had so many ways to dispose of bodies. You've heard of the 'cement shoes' on guys dumped in the river, and bodies have been found cemented into the foundations of old buildings and on and on. Maybe it was just Civella's way of immortalizing the infamous Jimmy Hoffa for his own purposes. Civella had his own problems, and if push ever came to shove, he could use Hoffa's body as his ace in the hole."

"You said that the authorities had Hoffa's DNA?"

"Yes, they do."

I knew it was a long shot, but what the hell? I called the captain and shared our theory. I suggested that they might run a comparison of the skeleton DNA with that of the missing Jimmy Hoffa.

To this day, I don't know if the comparison was ever run.

All I know is that the last call I made before boarding my flight back to Hawaii was to the brass running the case.

I foolishly asked if the body found in my building was the long-lost Jimmy Hoffa.

Their curt reply was, "At this point in our investigation, we cannot confirm or deny the identity of the victim."

What do you suppose that meant?

CHAPTER THIRTEEN

As I settled in on the long flight back to Kauai, I reviewed the events of the past year. They had unfolded like an old Mickey Spillane novel.

Maggie and I had been kidnapped, mugged, beaten, and nearly roasted; I feared more was to come, remembering the dire warning of Uncle Ray.

I silently wondered if Maggie was having any second thoughts. When we met we were both realtors, and the worst thing we had to endure was the wrath of an irate homeowner who was upset because his home hadn't sold yet.

She hadn't signed up to be Dale Evans to my Roy Rogers.

I had always imagined the golden years to be peaceful and serene, and I had pictured us walking hand-in-hand in exotic places and curled up together in front of a fire on a cold winter's night.

Instead, I had given her a steady flow of murder, mayhem, lowlifes, and scumbags.

She had every reason in the world to make a hasty exit—stage left.

These ruminations made for an uncomfortable ride back to paradise.

My fears, however justified, were allayed when Maggie greeted me at the terminal. There was no mistaking the absolute conviction of her hug as she threw herself into my arms and pressed tight against my body.

It brought to mind the old adage, "Worry is the interest paid on trouble that may never come due."

On the ride to the Marriott, I gave her the gory details of the mysterious skeleton in my closet, and she filled me in on what I had missed during my incarceration. It was comforting to hear that while Waimea Canyon and Hanalei Bay were beautiful, they lacked the one thing that would have made them perfect—me!

I wanted to stay up with Maggie, but my poor body that had crossed four time zones twice in three days suddenly shut down. My biological clock was so screwed up that the only apparent solution was to press the reset button, and I conked out.

When I awoke fourteen hours later, I thought maybe I had died and gone to heaven.

The warm sun was streaming in the window, and my beautiful bride-to-be was sitting by my bed with a room service tray filled with warm pastries, fresh fruit, and an omelet the size of a football. After partaking of this sumptuous feast, I showered and shaved and finally felt like I had rejoined the human race.

Maggie took my hand and led me to the living room, and we sat together on the couch.

"Walt, tomorrow is the big day. Unless you pull another crazy stunt, we may actually have a chance to be married, but I think I have something here you should see."

Maggie had shared with Sammy our misgivings about beginning our new life together amid the ruins of the hurricane-ravaged Coco Palms. There are hundreds of beautiful places in the islands where we could be married, and I had wondered several times why we had chosen this one.

"Sammy gave me these tapes," she said. "I think we should take a look."

The Coco Palms had been one of the premier Hawaiian resorts in the sixties. Its luxurious grounds with lagoons surrounded by two thousand palm trees was the perfect setting for the wedding scene in Elvis's *Blue Hawaii*.

Larry Rivera, a young boy during the filming of the movie, became close friends with Elvis and eventually became the featured performer at the resort's lounge.

The first tape featured Uncle Larry and his family performing for a huge crowd during the resort's glory years. We sat mesmerized, listening to Uncle Larry singing all the traditional Hawaiian favorites. We especially enjoyed the songs he had written: "Kamalai," "Beautiful Rainbow," and "Limahuli." We realized that a very special person was planning our wedding.

The second tape was Elvis's *Blue Hawaii*, which had been the catalyst for our decision to be married in Hawaii when we watched it weeks ago.

This time as we watched Chad and Maile exchange vows and glide down the beautiful lagoon together, we envisioned ourselves in that enchanted place, and somehow it all made sense again.

Finally, Maggie's words sealed the deal. "Walt, you have loved Elvis all your life. You rescued his lost tapes and helped introduce his music to a whole new generation. You performed his songs for thousands of people, and most importantly, you were the King when you asked me to be your wife. It just wouldn't be right any other way."

Is she special or what?

"And I have another surprise. Sammy is picking us up after lunch, and we're going to meet Uncle Larry at the Palms and tour the grounds."

Cool!

I'm not sure what I was expecting when we met Uncle Larry, but I certainly wasn't disappointed.

He was about our age, maybe a little older. He was small in stature, but you could tell right away that he had a heart as big as Mount Wai'ale'ale. He had lived on the island all his life, and we found him to be the embodiment of the spirit of aloha.

As we toured the grounds, the ruins came to life as he shared the stories of his youth. He pointed out the cottage where Elvis stayed during the filming of the movie and the rock wall he crawled over at night to meet the young Larry who showed him around the island. We stood in what was left of the hotel's showroom and could almost feel the ghosts of Frank Sinatra, Bing Crosby, and royalty from around the world. We imagined the famous torchlight ceremony that ushered in the evening's festivities for over forty years.

And suddenly the resort was no longer just the ruins left devastated by Iniki but a memorial to Hawaii's glorious past and a shrine to one of the most famous wedding scenes in cinematic history.

And we were going to be a part of it all.

I awoke early the next morning. Maggie was still deep in sleep when I slipped out of bed. I stood at the bedside and watched the rhythmic pattern of her breathing, her auburn tresses cascading over her face, and I marveled at how this lovely creature had come into my life.

In a few short hours she would become my wife, and we would spend our remaining years together.

I quietly slid open the door to the lanai and watched the first rays of the morning sun cast its golden splendor on the surface of the sea.

It seemed as if the gentle trade winds had blown the cobwebs from my mind and the sixty-seven years of my life lay spread out before me.

I saw the years of my youth spent on my grandparents' farm, the turbulent years of puberty and young adulthood when I struggled to find who I wanted to be, and the mundane but successful years as a realtor.

Then I saw my life change dramatically that day in the parking lot when a young thug assaulted an elderly woman.

In one short year, my life had been transformed from one of mere existence to one of purpose.

I reflected on what I had accomplished since enlisting in the army of Lady Justice, and the burning I felt deep in my bosom told me that I was doing what I was meant to do.

One never knows how many more years they will be given, but whatever that number will be, I know they will be well spent with the two most important women in my life.

As if to add confirmation to my reverie, I felt an arm slide around my waist and a warm body press against me, and we stood silently together watching the dawn of the first day of the rest of our lives together.

At last the time had come.

We met Willie and Mary by the pool.

The casual observer would never have guessed that we were a wedding party.

Willie had evidently done some shopping in my absence and was resplendent in a new aloha shirt covered with buxom girls perched seductively on surfboards. Not traditional wedding attire, but when in Rome.

Mary was decked out in a muumuu that had more flowers than a president's funeral. I hoped we wouldn't be attacked by a swarm of bees or hummingbirds.

In keeping with the Elvis *Blue Hawaii* wedding theme, I wore a white billowy shirt and white pants with a red sash around the waist, and Maggie wore a full-length lavender Hawaiian dress.

I wore a red lei around my neck, and Maggie had a white one made of the fragrant tuberose.

Our little group was colorful if nothing else.

Sammy picked us up at the bell desk. The car was strangely silent during the twenty-minute drive to the Coco Palms. I think we were all silently holding our collective breaths, wondering if this long awaited event was actually going to materialize or if fate would, once again, intervene to delay our special day.

When the car pulled into the parking area without incident, everyone breathed a sigh of relief.

We were really getting married!

Uncle Larry met us at the gate, and together we strolled down the path to the footbridge over the lagoon. Larry's wife and daughter were there with their instruments.

Beautiful arrangements of heleconia, anthurium, protea, and ginger added their vibrant hues to the lush tropical setting. Stately palms gently swayed with the ebb and flow of the gentle trade winds, and the lagoon reflected the azure blue of the cloudless sky.

Maggie squeezed my hand.

"It's just perfect," I heard her whisper.

Then I noticed another figure standing quietly to the side.

Uncle Larry had told us that while he would be putting the wedding together, he was not an ordained minister, so he would provide someone with the proper credentials to officiate the ceremony.

I'm not sure exactly what I was expecting, but this guy wasn't it.

He looked to be about my age. He was tall and gaunt. His scruffy salt-and-pepper beard matched his long hair that had been pulled back into a ponytail. His full, flowing robe touched the ground and was fastened by a rope tied loosely around his waist.

He looked like he had just spent the weekend at Woodstock.

He had, no doubt, seen our apprehension. He stepped forward, his hand extended, and simply said, "Aloha. I'm Reverend Winslow. I am honored to be a part of your special day."

As I took his hand and met the gaze of his clear blue eyes, I felt the same spirit that had surrounded

Uncle Larry the first time we met, and I instinctively knew that we were in good hands.

He led us to the center of the footbridge. Willie was on my left, Maggie was on my right, and Mary stood next to Maggie.

I had played this moment over and over in my mind a hundred times. I was only going to do this once, and I wanted it to be perfect.

It was.

I hadn't noticed that Reverend Winslow had carried a large conch shell onto the footbridge. He held the shell aloft.

"In Hawaii, sacred ceremonies begin by invoking the presence of the Great Spirit. We do this with the blowing of the conch. I will blow three times to invite the Great Spirit. In the marriage ceremony, the length of the third note will tell us the length of your time together. I will do my best to sustain many years for the two of you."

With that, he tilted his head and brought the shell to his lips.

We were all amazed at the clear, pure tone that resonated from the shell and seemed to drift heavenward on the warm tropical breeze.

He blew a second time, the note sustained for maybe ten seconds.

He lowered the shell momentarily, and as he filled his lungs with air, Maggie grabbed my hand and held it tight.

He pressed the shell to his lips a third time. Based on the first two notes, we expected this one to last maybe fifteen or twenty seconds, but we stood for what seemed like an eternity as the sacred tone pierced the air and reverberated through the swaying palms.

As the last of the note finally drifted away on the breeze, we were all speechless, except Mary, who summed it up for all of us when I heard her mutter under her breath, "Damn!"

Reverend Winslow continued, "In Hawaii, the seasons of the year are not as distinct as yours in Missouri. Having myself come to this beautiful place from the Midwest, I know, as you do, the promise that each season holds.

"In the spring, life bursts forth anew; flowers bloom, trees awaken from their sleep, and the seeds of new life are planted in all living things. It is a time of hope, a time to build dreams for the new year.

"Then come the long, warm days of summer, when those seeds, so lovingly planted, grow and mature and bear fruit. It is a time to cultivate and nurture, a time to strengthen.

"Soon come the glorious days of autumn, when we harvest the bounty we have nurtured and marvel at the wonders of nature as greens turn to crimson and gold. It is a time of thanksgiving and reflection for the blessings of life, a time to store away that which we have harvested for the long cold days of winter.

"And finally, when the winter winds of life blow and living things become still, if we have planted, nurtured, and harvested wisely, we will be sustained until life begins its cycle anew.

"For those uniting in matrimony, it is not unlike the seasons of the year.

"Those uniting in the springtime of their youth will know the joy of bringing forth new life and dreaming dreams of the seasons to come.

"They along with those who unite in the warm summer of their lives will know the joy of cultivating and nurturing that which will bring warmth and security and comfort for the seasons that lay ahead.

"Then there are those like you, Walt and Maggie, who come to be united in the autumn of your lives. While for you the season has passed to plant the seeds that will bring forth new life, your joining together today will give birth to a new entity that did not previously exist, an entity that must be nurtured and cultivated if it is to grow and prosper, an entity in which you may dream your dreams for the future and in which you may find your comfort in the winter years of your life.

"Autumn, again, is a time for thanksgiving and reflection, a time to enjoy the bounty of your life. So take the time to reflect on your past and be thankful for the circumstances of life that have brought you together. Embrace one another, love one another, and marvel at the crimson and gold of your autumn years together."

I heard a sniffle and looked at Willie just in time to see him wipe a tear from his cheek.

"Walt, please take Maggie's hand and repeat after me: I, Walter, take thee, Margaret, to be my wedded wife, to have and to hold from this day forward, for richer, for poorer, in sickness and in health, keeping myself from all others until death to us both shall part."

It's not my nature to get overly emotional, but it took all my inner resolve to utter those precious words without blubbering like an idiot.

As Maggie looked into my eyes and affirmed her vows to me, I felt like the luckiest man in the world.

I guess that's the way it's supposed to be.

Reverend Winslow continued, "Do you have your rings?"

I nodded at Willie, and he plunged his hand deep into his pocket. As his hand came out, the diamond setting caught in the fabric and flipped into the air.

It was like one of those movie scenes when everything seems to move in slow motion. We all gasped as the ring reached the apex of its arc and fell onto the narrow bridge over the lagoon.

It rolled, of course, as round things do, right to the edge of the footbridge. Its momentum was sufficient to carry it over the edge, but a small brown gecko that had chosen that moment to bask in the warm sun blocked its path into a watery grave.

I kneeled down to retrieve the ring, and I will swear to this day that the gecko winked at me as he sped away.

Once order had been restored, the reverend continued, "You have come to our beautiful islands to seal your marriage vows. In the past few days and the days to come, as you experience our soft sand beaches, our gentle trade winds fragrant with flowers and salt sea mist, and the warmth of our tropical sun, you are storing away precious memories that are yours to keep forever. Memories that in future days you may reflect upon, draw strength from, and give you joy.

"You have come to this beautiful sanctuary to affirm the marriage vows you have just made, with the exchange of rings.

"The wedding ring is a symbol of everlasting love, a circle, without beginning, without end. And the exchange of these rings is a pledge one to the other of the total commitment you have made and an outward sign to the world of your fidelity to each other.

"Walt, please take Maggie's hand and place the token of your love on her finger and repeat after me: With this ring, I pledge my everlasting love and seal the covenant I have made to you."

Maggie then turned to Mary, who promptly dug into the cleavage of her ample bosom and produced the ring that she held in a death grip. She wasn't about to tempt fate a second time.

After Maggie had sealed her covenant with my ring, Reverend Winslow concluded the ceremony. "May your love for each other be as the rings you have given: pure, untarnished, and without end. You may seal your pledge with a kiss."

As I took Maggie into my arms and our lips met, the words from "The Hawaiian Wedding Song" filled the air:

> This is the moment
> I've waited for
> I can feel my heart singing.

My heart was indeed singing. I was standing with the love of my life by my side in the very spot that fifty years ago Elvis had stood and sung those very words.

It was a moment that was indelibly pressed between the pages of my mind and one that in years to come would bring me untold joy and happiness.

Uncle Larry and his family sang and played, and Mary snapped dozens of photos while we shared little pieces of wedding cake. Arbor Mist Tropical Fruit had replaced the traditional champagne, at my request, of course. It goes well with everything.

Too soon it had to end.

I took Maggie in my arms, and we danced our wedding dance to the beautiful "Can't Help Falling in Love."

At last Maggie and I were one.

CHAPTER FOURTEEN

D ue to my brief incarceration, our wedding day was to be our last on the island of Kauai. In fact, we had to arrange for a late checkout to accommodate the ceremony. Sammy rushed us to the airport just in time to catch our island hop to Maui.

It wasn't exactly how we had planned our honeymoon, and something in the back of my mind whispered that this was probably just the harbinger of things to come in our new life together. We could plan until the cows come home, but there were forces out there making plans for us as well.

Their plans, it would seem, trumped ours.

As the plane descended into the Kahului airport, it was quite apparent why it was called the Valley Isle.

On the north side of the island were the West Maui Mountains, and on the south, the massive bulk of the dormant volcano Haleakala rose ten thousand feet. The two were connected by a valley that stretched from sea to sea.

Although the sun was shining brightly, the summit of the majestic volcano was shrouded in misty clouds, and I was suddenly overcome with the eerie feeling that our lives were somehow inextricably bound to the mysterious past of this mountain that had once been the home of Pele, the goddess of fire.

As we descended the steps to the baggage claim area, we were met by a smiling Hawaiian man who stepped forward with the traditional plumeria leis. "Aloha, my name is Liho, and I'm—"

"Let me guess," I interrupted, "you're a cousin to Buddy Kalakoa."

"How'd you guess that?" he said with a grin. "Let's get your bags and get you to your hotel."

During the drive from the airport through the city of Kahului, it was obvious that this was the commercial center of the island. We passed all of the mainland big box stores like Costco and Walmart, and we were relieved to see that the islanders had not been deprived of the culinary delights offered by the likes of Krispy Kreme and Mickey D's.

The sprawl of the city ended abruptly, and the one highway to the west side of the island was soon surrounded by fields of sugarcane and pineapple.

It took a mere twenty minutes to drive from the east to the west side of the island, and after passing by the Maui Ocean Center and a shopping area located on Maalaea Bay, we pulled off the road and parked at what Liho called "McGregor Point."

The scene that awaited us was the epitome of what one would expect the definition of a tropical paradise to be.

The small pinnacle of land that was the point jutted out into the blue waters of the bay. On the left, all of south Maui was visible against the backdrop of Mt. Haleakala. The ridges of the Molokini cinder cone and the island of Kahoolawe lay straight ahead, and the island of Lanai loomed across the western sea.

We all stood in awe, basking in the warm sun as the trade winds lifted the salt sea mist from the waves that crashed on the rocky shore.

Mary, as always, summed up what we were all feeling. "Damn! I could get used to this!"

The ride along the west side of the island was beautiful. The highway ran parallel to the ocean shore, and at some locations it was so close that the breaking waves left their salty residue on the pavement.

We passed through the old whaling village of Lahaina to the resort area known as Kaanapali.

The mile-long stretch of Kaanapali Beach is lined with resorts, luxury condominiums, shopping centers, and restaurants and has become a permanent fixture in the list of the top ten beaches in the world. Liho explained that while our hotel, the Kaanapali Beach Hotel, was one of the original resorts in the area, it differed from the glitz and glamour of some of the newer resorts. It is billed as "Hawaii's Most Hawaiian Hotel."

I could tell the difference the minute we stepped into the lobby. I felt as if I had stepped into a time machine that had taken us back thirty years to a simpler and more peaceful time.

Photos of Hawaiian kings, queens, and princesses adorned the walls. Feathered *kahilis* and wooden drums set among arrangements of tropical flowers accented the elegant but understated décor.

A beautiful Hawaiian woman with long, flowing black hair approached us. "Aloha, I am Noelani. Welcome to our hotel."

Noelani, it turned out, was a cousin to Liho, who, of course, was a cousin to Buddy.

Why was I not surprised?

"Let's get you checked into your rooms so you can freshen up before dinner."

The hotel formed a giant U, with the restaurant, pool, and tiki bar in the center. The hotel rooms faced inward toward the beautifully manicured grounds and the ocean. The rooms at the end of the U were separated from the beach only by a concrete walkway that ran for a mile along the entire Kaanapali resort.

I couldn't believe that one of these special rooms was ours.

We quickly unpacked our bags and stepped onto the lanai. Frothy waves broke onto the beach a mere fifty feet from where we stood. Neither of us wanted to end this magic moment, but we just had time to wash off the travel grime before supper.

Willie and Mary were sharing a room next to us. We met and strolled together to the elegant restaurant that faced the tiki bar and a small stage.

After a sumptuous meal of mahi mahi encrusted with macadamia nuts, the lights in the courtyard dimmed, and from somewhere in the darkness a plaintive voice that seemed to span the ages lifted an ancient chant into the night air.

As the chant came closer, the figure of a man wielding a lighted torch approached and touched the flame to other torches surrounding the courtyard. Soon the area was bathed in the flickering torchlight.

Another figure appeared from the shadows. It was a Hawaiian woman in a ti leaf skirt who began to sway to the rhythm of the chant.

In the brighter light, I recognized our new friends, Liho and Noelani.

The torchlight ceremony was followed by a hula show that had been a nightly fixture at the hotel for many years.

Liho and Noelani performed both the traditional Hawaiian hulas and the *hapa-haoule* hulas made famous in the movies.

We enjoyed the hulas sung in English such as "The Little Grass Shack" and "We're Going to a Hukilau," but the ancient chants, sung in Hawaiian, struck a chord deep in my soul. As I listened, the vision of Maggie and I tied to a stake with a burning torch poised over our heads filled my mind. The eerie chant that came from the lips of the man bent on sacrificing us to his gods was not unlike that sung by our friend Liho.

After the hula show, the trio onstage played all the Hawaiian favorites. While Maggie and I twirled on the tiny dance floor in front of the stage, Mary busied herself collecting umbrellas from more fruity drinks than I could ever hold, and Willie found a willing lass seated at the tiki bar.

All was well in paradise.

Finally, the band announced their final number, and the audience drifted away, leaving the courtyard to the serious drinkers around the bar.

Mary, I noticed, was listing heavily to starboard; her chin was propped on one elbow, and a silly grin was plastered across her face.

I feared she had gone a few umbrellas past her limit.

I looked around for Willie, hoping to get some help in getting our inebriated friend back to her room, but he was nowhere to be seen.

Mary struggled to her feet, and with Maggie on one side and me on the other, we staggered down the path to her room.

The steps to the second floor landing proved to be a challenge, and we stood huffing and puffing outside her door.

"Key?" I queried.

All I got was a dumb look. I don't think I was speaking Hawaiian, but I might as well have been as far as Mary was concerned.

She wasn't carrying a purse, and having seen on other occasions where she hid things for safekeeping, I had a pretty good idea where the key might be. But there was no way in hell that I was going to go fishing around in her cleavage for a door key.

It occurred to me that Willie might have tired and come back to the room ahead of us, and I was about to knock when I noticed a sock over the doorknob.

"What the heck is that?" I asked, looking at Maggie.

"I don't know. Maybe somebody dropped it in the hall and thought it might belong to the occupant of this room. Your guess is as good as mine."

I shrugged and knocked on the door. There was no response, but I was sure I had heard movement inside the room.

I knocked louder this time, thinking maybe Willie had been asleep and my gentle knock had only roused him to semi-consciousness.

Still no answer, so I knocked even louder and called his name. "Willie, wake up!"

I thought I heard a whisper and footsteps, and soon the door opened just a crack.

"What you want?" Willie growled. "Din you see my sign?"

"Sign? What sign?"

"De sock! Din you see de sock?"

"Well, yeah. Is that supposed to mean something to me?"

"Shit, man. Everbody knows dat a sock on de knob means you is entertainin' a lady. Now go away."

"Can't do it, man. You see, we've got us a situation here." I pointed to Mary, who was hanging on to the doorjamb for dear life with drool running down her chin.

"Oh, man, I was jus' gettin' to de good part. Can't you take her to your room?"

"Willie, this is my wedding night, and there's no way in hell that I'm going to share it with Mary Murphy, so open the door."

"Hang on," he whimpered. He retreated, and I heard a few hushed whispers, some pleading and begging, and finally a firm, "No! Goodnight!"

The door burst open, whacking Mary in the head, and the woman Willie was romancing at the bar slipped quietly into the night.

Mary's bed was closest to the open lanai, and with great effort we drug her across the floor and plopped her onto the mattress. Maggie tucked her in, and as we were heading out the door, I pulled Willie aside.

"Thanks, Willie. I appreciate the sacrifice."

"Yeah, well, I wouldn't do it for no one but you, but what a waste. Now what am I gonna do with dis?" He looked down at the huge protrusion straining the seams of his Levi's.

"I'm sure you'll think of something," I muttered as I ushered Maggie quickly out the door.

Having deposited our excess baggage, we found ourselves alone again on the Kaanapali beach walkway.

The cool breeze off the ocean brought the sound of the waves washing onto the sand, and as each wave crested and fell, the silver moonlight danced ever so briefly then disappeared, waiting for the next swell.

"How about a walk along the beach?" I suggested.

Maggie didn't need any coaxing, and soon we were standing barefoot in the sand as the incoming tide swirled around our ankles.

We walked hand-in-hand through the surf, and occasionally we could see the running lights of some small craft poking red and green holes in the darkness of the vast ocean.

On the shore, the lights from the resorts reflected in the water, and from some restaurant down the beach, the melody of a Hawaiian song danced across the water to the rhythm of the waves.

There was no one but us along the beach, and in a weak moment, the love scene in *From Here To Eternity* where Burt Lancaster took Deborah Kerr right there in the sand as the waves washed over them popped into my mind.

I was thinking how incredibly romantic that would be, just Maggie and I consummating our wedding vows right there on the beach, when an unusually strong wave sent the frigid water up my leg, soaking my private parts.

I knew right away as I felt Mr. Winkie making a hasty retreat that such nonsense was better left to Hollywood.

Shrunken but not discouraged, I held Maggie close and whispered, "You feel like going to a nookie-lau?"

That goofy play on words had been rattling around in my mind all evening after hearing the real version at the hotel. I had been busting to say it all night, and at last the time seemed right.

Romantic cuss, aren't I?

She stood on tiptoes and whispered back, "Are you wanting to spend some time in my little grass shack?"

That got Mr. Winkie's attention right away.

We hustled back to our room. Maggie told me to get comfortable and disappeared into the bathroom.

The door opened, and she demurely stepped into the room wearing a sheer black teddy that was just long enough for the black fur in the hem to cover—well, it just barely covered it.

"I did some shopping while you were on the mainland. Do you like it?" she purred.

"Like it? Are you kidding?"

I felt like a kid in a candy store. No, wait. It was more like a kid on Christmas morning anxiously awaiting the moment when he could remove the wrapping and finally hold in his hands the special gift that had been given him.

Maggie came to me and climbed on my lap. I brought her close to me and had just began to nuzzle into that soft black fur when—

"*Yieeaahh!*" The most bloodcurdling scream I had ever heard this side of a slasher movie pierced the air.

That will take the wind out of your sails every time.

I jumped to my feet, nearly throwing Maggie on the floor. "Quick! Throw something on. I think that came from Mary's room."

"*Yieeaah!* Somebody help!"

I rushed into the hall, and without stopping to knock, I hit the door with all my adrenaline-pumped strength.

The doorframe shattered, and I stepped into a scene from the *Twilight Zone*.

Willie was standing wide-eyed on the side of his bed, his white sheet pulled up around his chin.

Mary was sitting straight up in her bed pointing to the screen door of the lanai that had been left partly open.

I followed her frantic stare, and there, silhouetted against the moonlit sky, was a great horned beast.

Maggie was close behind. We saw the creature at the same time. She grabbed my arm and pulled me back.

"What is that thing?" she gasped.

I, of course, had no idea, and I was just trying to decide how brave I wanted to be on my wedding night before I had had the opportunity to consummate our union when Liho stepped up behind us.

Apparently Mary's screams had jarred more than one guest out of their beds.

"What's up?" he asked.

I just pointed to the horned specter clinging to the screen mere inches from Mary's terrified face.

Liho flipped on the lights, and a big grin spread across his face.

"Hey, man. What you got there is a Jackson's chameleon. It won't hurt you." He crossed the room, and we all looked on in horror as he gently pried the creature from the screen. "They look tough, but they just eat bugs."

Mary finally spoke. "I thought I was having the DTs, and then that damn thing started coming at me. I ain't never going to drink that much again. I promise."

I took a closer look at the big lizard. It measured maybe twelve inches. It sure looked bigger in the dark. It had three big horns like a triceratops. Who wouldn't have been scared by that?

Two huge eyes protruded from the side of his head. Each of them could rotate 180 degrees independently, and as Liho held him up, he surveyed each of us and was probably wondering what all the fuss was about.

Willie hadn't moved a muscle. He just stood there with the sheet pulled up around his chin. Finally, he said, "Dat crazy old bat done scared de bejesus outta me. Den I saw dat ting, and den she screamed again. I think I wet myself."

"The worst thing he could do is lick you to death," Liho said as he headed to the door. "His tongue is a foot and a half long."

Willie considered that for a minute, and as he climbed out of the bed, I heard him mutter, "I bet Emma would like one of dem."

I wonder what he meant by that.

After everyone was tucked safely back in bed, Maggie and I returned to our room.

"Well, it's been quite a day," I said.

I was about to apologize when Maggie put her finger to my lips.

"Walter Williams, I knew what I was getting into when I agreed to marry you. Our life together may never be predictable, but it will never be dull. We're in it together, for better or for worse, right?"

"Right."

"Now get over here."

"Yes, ma'am."

CHAPTER FIFTEEN

What a night!

After our nocturnal encounter with the great horned beast, sleep didn't come easy. The sun was high in the sky by the time we convened for breakfast.

Mary looked like the old mare that had been ridden hard and put away wet, and she kept repeating over and over, "Don't give me no more umbrellas, please!"

Willie was unusually quiet. His romantic tryst had been interrupted, and his bravado had been shaken. He was the perfect candidate for the next installment of *Grumpy Old Men*.

Maggie and I were exhausted as well, but for other reasons. Try as I might, I couldn't wipe the silly grin off my face.

A pot of hot coffee, fresh papaya, and waffles smothered in coconut syrup made a world of difference.

We had just left the restaurant and were headed to the gift shop in the lobby when two men approached us.

"Mr. Williams, my name is Detective Chinn. I wonder if we could have a word with you?"

I looked at Maggie, and she gave me that what-have-you-done-now stare.

"Uh, sure," I replied. "What's this all about?"

"We were hoping you could help us."

"Help you do what?"

"Help us with an undercover operation."

I just stood there dumbfounded. "How do you even know me?"

"Well, actually, you're somewhat of a celebrity. We know about your involvement with the stolen artifacts."

"Don't tell me. You're related to Buddy Kalakoa."

"On my mother's side."

"But I just got married yesterday. This is my honeymoon. I didn't come here to work."

"Come on, Harry," the other detective said. "We knew he wouldn't help."

Mary giggled. "Did you say Harry? Your name is Harry Chinn?"

I rolled my eyes and buried my face in my hands. "I'm sorry, man. She had a few too many mai tais last night."

"Hey, I get that all the time. You've heard the Johnny Cash tune, 'A Boy Named Sue.' Well, with a name like that, I had to get tough or die. That's why I'm a cop."

I figured anybody that liked Johnny Cash couldn't be all bad.

"I know I'm going to regret this. What's on your mind?"

"We have our fair share of crime here in the islands—you know, domestic stuff, people beating the crap out of each other, and crystal meth is a major problem—but most damaging to the tourist industry is petty theft. Tourists rent a car, throw their luggage in the trunk, and head to their resort. They stop along the beach to wade in the surf, and when they come back, their luggage is gone.

"We warn people from the get-go, 'Don't leave valuables in your car,' but it's so easy to leave your camera and wallet in the car when you go for a swim. The bad guys know that."

"So what do you want from us?"

"Well, I took the liberty of calling your captain—"

"Captain Short is in on this?"

"Well," he said with a sly grin, "he did say that back in Kansas City you had quite a reputation for your undercover work. You know, the tranny bar and all."

"No T-shirt for the captain," I muttered.

"Anyway, we hoped that you would help us out. Your little group is perfect for our sting."

"How so?"

"Well, look at you. You reek of tourist. Gaudy shirt, Bermuda shorts, tennis shoes with white socks, and lily-white legs. You're perfect."

I wasn't sure whether that was a compliment or an insult.

"Here's the deal. We'll give you everything: rental car, camera, tote bags full of stuff. All you have to do is go to the beach and have a good time and leave your stuff in the car. Our guys will be watching, and when they hit your car, we'll nab them."

"I don't know. It's been a pretty tough week."

"Yeah, we know all about your mix-up back on the mainland. Tell you what. I'll sweeten the pot for you. My wife's brother works at the Old Lahaina Luau. Give us a hand, and I think I can score four front row tickets for you."

I looked at my little group.

"We haven't been to a luau yet," Maggie whispered.

"Yeah, and I been wanting to see one of those fire dancer guys," Mary added.

Willie just shrugged his shoulders.

Seeing no opposition, I turned to Harry Chinn.

"I guess we're in."

"Great! Go pack your swimming gear and meet us in front of the hotel."

In fifteen minutes we were packed and ready to go. Detective Chinn was standing beside a brand new Chrysler Sebring convertible.

"You've got to be kidding," I stammered.

"Nope. This is the rental car of choice for the yuppie elite. They come from cold places like Chicago. They've never even owned a convertible and figure their Hawaiian vacation is the perfect place to let it all hang out. There's a bazillion of these on Maui. Next time you see one, look who's behind the wheel."

"So what's the plan?"

"Did you stop at McGregor Point on the way over?"

"Sure did. It was gorgeous."

"Well, so does everyone else. They have spotters there who check out the newest greenhorns on the island. If they spot a patsy, they follow them along the highway. After you go through the tunnel, the first beach that is accessible from the highway is at Ukumehame. It's a good bet that Mr. and Mrs. Tourist will pull over for their first taste of Hawaiian sand and surf. That's when they strike."

"So what do you want us to do?"

"Drive past McGregor Point, and turn around at the Ocean Center. Then come back and stop just as if you were coming from the airport. Ooh and ah and get all excited just like you did when you stopped before; then drive to the beach at Ukumehame. We'll show you the spot on the way over. Leave your stuff in the open convertible, take a swim, and enjoy the ocean. We'll do the rest."

"Piece of cake."

"Oh, by the way, there was a storm several hundred miles out, so the surf's a bit high today. Be careful."

We followed our instructions to the letter and pulled off the highway and parked under a gnarly old kiawe tree. We grabbed our swim gear and headed for the beach, leaving the camera and other gear supplied by the cops in plain sight.

Sure enough, the gentle waves that had swirled around our ankles the day before were now rolling onto the beach chest high. At first we were timid about venturing into the surf, but after a few trial runs, we found it exhilarating and were soon body surfing onto the sandy beach.

I have no idea how long we splashed in the water. As the old saying goes, "Time flies when you're having fun."

After a while Maggie and Willie and I were absolutely waterlogged and headed for the beach towels and sand mats to catch our breath.

Mary was having none of it.

"Hell no, I ain't coming in. In a few days I'm gonna be back at that damn hotel and wishing I was here. And when do you suppose I'll ever be back? Huh?

Never! That's when! So you all go rest. I'm gonna surf till I drop."

She didn't know how prophetic that would be.

The three of us sat on our mats lathering up with sunscreen thoroughly enjoying Mary splashing and bobbing in the thundering waves. The surf had continued to rise during our time there, and every so often a set bordering on scary would hit the beach.

Mary had finally had enough, and as I watched her stagger to her feet and slosh toward the shore, the retreating surf seemed to slide back into the ocean farther than usual.

Mary had just raised her hand to wave to us when I saw it coming.

I jumped to my feet and screamed a warning, but it was too late.

A wall of foaming blue water ten feet tall blasted into Mary's backside, pitching her forward, face first, into the sand. The huge wave then thundered over her, sweeping her onto the beach like a rag doll.

Once its fury was spent, it retreated into the depths as quickly as it had come, leaving Mary beached like a dead whale.

We rushed to her side.

"Mary! Mary! Are you all right?"

We lifted her into a sitting position. She hacked and coughed, spit sea water and sand. When at last she was able to speak, her first word was "Damn!" followed closely by, "Maybe I need one of those umbrella things after all."

Detective Chinn had witnessed the whole affair and came running down the beach.

"Is she okay?"

"I think so. She wants another mai tai, so that's probably a good sign."

"You have just learned rule number one: never turn your back on the ocean."

"And rule number two?"

"Never swim in murky water. Unless, of course, you want to be lunch for a shark."

"We'll keep that in mind. How did the sting go? We never heard any commotion."

"Dry run here. But wouldn't you know it, while we were watching you, they struck at Luanipoko Beach a few miles up the road."

"And I presume they got away clean?"

"Sure did. As a matter of fact, their target was a couple from your neck of the woods, Kansas City."

"No kidding?"

Harry pulled out his notebook. "Yeah, the gal's name was Florence Wingate, and her boyfriend's name was Rocky Graham. The perps really cleaned them out. Took all their luggage: wallet, purse, everything. By the time they discovered the loss, the perps had maxed out two credit cards."

Hmmm, Florence Wingate, I thought. The name sounded familiar, but I just couldn't place it.

Then Mary spoke up. "Mr. Walt, you remember that new tenant at the hotel, you know, the computer guy. The one whose wife ran off with all his stuff while he was in the hospital. I think her name was Florence."

Then it all came back to me. Mary was right on. I remembered Lawrence saying that his ex was somewhere in Hawaii, living the good life.

Immediately, my mind went to the second most important lady in my life, Lady Justice. Some skeptics say there is no justice in this old world, but somehow, the blind lady keeps the scales of life in balance. I couldn't wait to get home and tell Lawrence.

I tried not to let Harry Chinn see how pleased I was that the perps had made at least one more getaway.

"Sorry about that, Harry. Too bad they didn't hit us. Just the wrong place at the wrong time."

"Yeah, it happens. You guys did your part. Tourists all the way. Just take the Sebring back to the hotel, and I'll pick it up later when I drop off your tickets."

"We may stop for a bite of lunch. Any suggestions?"

"If you want something quick and simple, try Cool Cats. It's in Lahaina on the south end of Front Street right across from the big banyan tree."

Cool Cats was just my kind of place. A life-size cardboard cutout of Elvis was the first thing I saw as we climbed the stairs to the second floor of the open-air shopping center.

We were seated by the rail overlooking the huge banyan tree that covered a whole city block, and in the distance we could see the boats bobbing up and down in Lahaina Harbor.

The huge tree, planted in the 1800s, was sixty feet tall and covered two-thirds of an acre. Its multiple trunks and branches, some just a few feet off the ground, provided a shady respite from the warm Lahaina sun.

The sandwiches on the menu were named after cool people. I had a James Dean, Maggie had a Marilyn Monroe, and Willie had a Sammy Davis. I'm not sure what Mary ordered, but after her recent debacle, it should have been the Three Stooges.

Shortly after being seated, a grizzled old Hawaiian man peddled his ancient bicycle to the corner directly across from us. He removed a ukulele from the saddle-bag and began to sing and play. I couldn't distinguish the words, but he certainly sang with passion. After a few songs, he put the uke away and brought out his Bible. With all the fervor of a TV evangelist, he began to preach. No one stopped to listen. Actually, passersby gave him a wide berth, but that didn't deter him in the slightest.

I asked our waitress about the colorful old gent.

"Oh, that's Nathan. He lives on the other side of the island. He rides his bike here and preaches every day. He's been doing it as long as I can remember."

I watched fascinated, and every so often our eyes would meet. Even though I couldn't understand his words, he seemed to be speaking directly to me.

I was still hungry after my James Dean, so I ordered a big chocolate milkshake and two straws to share with Maggie.

Mary, though, was through.

"Hey, Mr. Walt, see that T-shirt shop right across from where we parked our car? I'm gonna go there and buy some cheap shirts for the boys at the hotel. Pick me up there when you finish your shake." And off she went.

We sat and slurped our shake and watched as Mary unfolded every shirt in the shop. She eventually tired of harassing the shirt guy and moved to the next store that sold all kinds of touristy trinkets. She was currently examining a huge coconut that could be addressed and mailed back to jealous friends on the mainland.

I had just settled our bill when I saw two guys lingering a bit too long around our car. I pointed them out to Willie and Maggie. "I think we may have trouble."

Sure enough, they hit the convertible with lightning speed and had our stuff scooped up in their arms in an instant.

"Maggie! You call Harry Chinn."

I leaned over the rail and yelled, "Hey! Put that stuff down!" Like that was going to do any good.

Of course they took off in different directions with our stuff clutched tightly in their arms.

My warning did, however, get the attention of one Mary Murphy.

One of the thieves had taken off down the sidewalk and would pass directly by the store where Mary was standing.

With impeccable timing, Mary swung the coconut right into the forehead of the fleeing thief.

Whock! You could hear the impact a block away. The poor thief, whose hands were full, never had a chance to defend himself.

Mary stood proudly over her vanquished foe and, smiling, gave me a big thumbs-up.

The other guy had sprinted under the banyan tree and would soon be out of sight. I motioned to Willie to follow me.

The thief had just reached the harbor street, and we saw him turn left. I told Willie to circle the block to his left while I pursued. Maybe we could cut him off. By the time we reached the street level, he had a sizeable lead. Knowing my limitations, I knew I could never catch him on foot.

Then I saw it.

"Nathan, I need to borrow your bike. I'll bring it right back."

Before he could utter a word of protest, I was peddling frantically after the thief.

I turned the corner by the harbor and saw him at the end of the next block by the old fort.

He saw me coming and turned left, back toward Front Street.

When I reached the point where I saw him turn, I saw that Willie had indeed cut him off, and he was standing on the sidewalk at the edge of the great tree.

Seeing Willie advancing from Front Street and me peddling from the harbor, he had only one avenue of escape left—through the labyrinth of the banyan tree.

He was obviously tiring from running with his arms loaded with booty, and we were gaining fast. Running at full tilt, he turned briefly to check our distance, which proved to be a costly mistake.

He turned back just in time to be clothes-lined by a low hanging branch of the banyan tree.

The tree didn't give an inch, and the luckless thief lay unconscious amid our scattered possessions.

I heard cop cars screaming up Front Street, and Harry Chinn hopped out of the car in time to see Mary Murphy with her foot on one luckless thief's throat and Willie Duncan straddling the other one.

Detective Chinn was impressed.

"Williams, you and your friends certainly lived up to your billing. We can't thank you enough. If there is anything we can do to make your visit more pleasant, please don't hesitate to ask. Here are your tickets. I hope you enjoy the luau."

Tired but happy, we trudged back toward our car. I pushed the old bicycle back to the corner where Nathan stood, watching and waiting. Sheepishly I said, "Thanks for the use of your bike. I didn't mean to be rude, but it was kind of an emergency."

He stared at me for the longest time then finally spoke, "Kamamalu, we will see one another again. You, Hualani, and I have much to do."

He climbed on his bike and rode away.

CHAPTER SIXTEEN

The Old Lahaina Luau was everything we hoped it would be.

The location was every man's dream of a tropical paradise. We arrived just in time to see the fiery red orb of the sun sink into the sea, and tiki torches lighted our path past grass huts and wooden canoes. We watched Hawaiian men uncover the emu and pull the pig, head and all, from the pit.

Mary was horrified and declared, "Ain't no way I'm eating none of that thing!"

But little umbrella drinks were free for the taking, and after taking far more than she should have, she threw caution to the wind and actually went back for three helpings of the succulent pig.

The show—featuring dancers from Hawaii, Fiji, New Zealand, and Tahiti—was fabulous.

The entire experience was quite obviously designed to appeal to the average tourists' misconception of life in Hawaii, but, hey, we were tourists after all, and we loved every minute of it.

Before the show we had met with Liho. He had said that if we were up for it, he would take us to one of the most spectacular scenes on the whole island—sunrise over the summit of the Haleakala Crater.

He explained that the conditions had to be just right—low clouds below the summit and clear skies above. The rising sun would burst through the clouds and illuminate the surreal landscape with breathtaking beauty.

But there was one catch—we had to leave at 4:00 a.m. to be at the summit by sunrise.

I had looked at my little group and could see without asking that as exciting as that sounded, we just weren't up for it.

We still wanted to see the crater, so Liho agreed to pick us up at nine for the trip up the mountain.

He told us to be sure to bring warm clothing, which prompted Mary to retort, "What do I need with warm clothing for? I didn't bring no warm clothes. It's ninety degrees out there."

Miss Tact all the way.

Liho patiently pointed out that at an altitude of ten thousand feet, the average temperature was in the fifties, and often the wind chill dipped into the thirties. Occasionally, snow would even fall in the winter.

So we "borrowed" blankets from our hotel room and met Liho in the lobby.

It was an hour drive from our hotel back to Kahului. Although the summit was only ten thousand feet, it was a thirty-seven mile journey from Kahului along the hairpin turns and switch backs to the top of the crater.

As we climbed from the valley floor into the foothills, the first little town we came to was called Pukalani.

Mary jumped on that one right away, "Pukalani! How'd they ever come up with a name like that?"

The ever-patient Liho responded, "It all has to do with the geography of the mountain. Our trade winds and our weather come from the east side of the island. The massive bulk of the mountain catches and holds the rain clouds, so the east side of the mountain is all lush rainforests.

"Because the rain clouds are trapped on the east side, the west side receives very little rain and resembles your western deserts.

"Pukalani is right in between. A few miles to the east in Makawao; it rains almost every day. A few miles to the west, cacti grow on barren hillsides. The literal translation of Pukalani is 'hole in the heavens.' It has just the right amount of rain and sunshine.

"Say, we've been driving for an hour and a half, and it's another hour and a half to the summit. Anybody up for a snack?"

Receiving an enthusiastic yes, Liho pulled into the parking lot of the Pukalani Superette. "They've got snacks and drinks in here, so help yourself. I'm going to get some *tako poke*."

"I like tacos too," Mary blurted. "Could you get me some?"

"Uh, sure, if that's what you want."

We all came back with chips and soft drinks and Twinkies, your typical *haole* junk food.

Liho joined us and handed a sack to Mary.

"I hope they put lots of cheese on them. I love cheese," she said as she opened the sack. "Holy mother of God! This ain't tacos! What is this awful stuff?"

We all looked at the plastic container that Mary held in her lap and instantly turned away with a collective, "Eww."

It was comforting to know that my gag reflex was in fine working order.

Liho was crestfallen. "It's *tako poke*. Just what you asked for."

"But what is it?"

"It's octopus mixed with herbs and spices. Hawaiian soul food. It's delicious."

Well, that certainly explained the little sucker things sticking up.

Liho popped the lid off his poke, and a smell that I can best describe as the bottom of a garbage can filled the car.

We all bailed out like kids doing a Chinese fire drill.

I tapped on Liho's window. "When you're through eating, let us know. We'll just wait out here."

We drove with the windows down, and it still took twenty minutes to clear the air of that awful stench.

As we drove up the mountain, we passed through pristine forests, and the *poke* smell was replaced by another sweet fragrance.

Maggie picked it up right away. "Um, what's that wonderful fragrance?"

"Eucalyptus," Liho replied. "This whole forest is eucalyptus."

As we wound up the switch backs, the forests turned to grassy fields where cows grazed along the road. We passed through low clouds that hugged the side of the mountain, and like a plane ascending in the sky, we broke through into brilliant sunshine.

The grassy fields gave way to rocky, barren hillsides where the vegetation was nearly nonexistent. We rounded another hairpin turn, and there alongside of the road was one of the most beautiful plants I had ever seen.

Growing there in that barren landscape was a flowering plant that stood at least six feet tall. Its massive base supported a stalk with hundreds of white blossoms.

"What is that?"

"That is *ahinahina*, the silversword," Liho replied. "It is a plant that grows only on the slopes of Haleakala. It only blooms once then dies. The blossoms drop seeds that start the next generation."

We looked around and saw smaller versions of the beautiful plant in various stages of growth.

"You have a very special mountain," I said.

"Indeed we do," he replied.

When we reached the summit, the sun was shining brightly in the cloudless blue sky. But when we stepped out of the car, it felt more like an October morning in Missouri than a summer day in Hawaii. We wrapped our purloined blankets around us and made fast tracks for the warmth of the visitor's center.

The center was built on the very edge of the crater rim, and the minute we stepped up to the window, the panoramic view of the Haleakala caldera took our breath away.

It felt like I had been riding in the Apollo 11 spacecraft and, with Neil Armstrong and Buzz Aldrin, found myself looking at the barren moonscape for the first time.

The crater rim was miles across, and below, massive cinder cones rose from the crater floor.

Liho stood by our side, and even though he had been here many times, I could still see the wonder in his eyes.

"The last eruption was in 1790. It has been dormant since. My people were coming here for a thousand years before that to pay homage to their gods. They called this place *wao akua*, the wilderness of the gods. It was the home of Pele, the goddess of fire.

"Many lives were sacrificed here to appease the angry gods, and noble kings, the *alii*, were laid to rest in the caves formed by lava tubes. It is a place of great *mana*."

"The artifacts that were recently stolen," I asked, "were they found here?"

"Many gravesites have been found over the years. There are hundreds of caves on the sheer inner face of the crater. And yes, they came from here, but only a few know its exact location. There are many of my people who believe the old bones should not be disturbed."

"And how do you feel about that?"

He thought for a moment. "It is not my place to say."

I was about to press our guide further when Willie pointed to the floor of the crater.

"Is dat people walkin' down der?"

Obviously relieved at the abrupt change in subject matter, Liho replied, "Yes, that's the Sliding Sands Trail. You can actually hike from the parking lot just over there, across the floor of the crater and out the other side. See that V in the crater wall on the other side? That's Kaupo Gap, and there is a trail that leads out of the crater through the gap to the other side of the island. Let me show you."

He led us to the center of the room to a large scale model of the crater. The many trails crisscrossing the park were clearly marked.

"What are these little dots along the trail?" I asked.

"Those are primitive cabins that can be rented. It is nearly impossible to hike the trail in a day, so hikers stay in the cabins and complete the hike the next day."

Our little group split up to look at the various displays, but I was drawn back to the window and stood gazing into the caldera when Maggie stepped up beside me.

She took my hand and stood close by my side.

"I can almost see the molten lava bubbling in the cauldron below," I said. "And I can imagine the ancient Hawaiians gathered here on this very spot, dancing and chanting and offering their sacrifices to Pele."

Maggie slid her arm around my waist. "So it's not just me then. If what Uncle Ray said was true, I could be related to one of those people who worshipped here or related to one who is buried somewhere out there on that cliff face."

I felt her shiver, and I pulled her closer.

Suddenly there appeared on the eastern edge of the crater rim a dark black cloud. It quickly swept across the mouth of the crater, and within minutes the sun that had shone so brightly was blotted out. The wind swirled around the visitor's center, and rain pelted against the glass.

"We need to get back down the mountain," Liho said.

By the time we reached the car, the temperature had dropped another ten degrees, and the car shook against the impact of the blustery winds.

As we drove away from the summit, something in the pit of my stomach told me that we had not seen the last of Madame Pele and the Haleakala Crater.

CHAPTER SEVENTEEN

We were exhausted after our mountaintop excursion and opted to just enjoy a good meal and a quiet evening, so we headed to old Lahaina Town. We parked in the pay lot by Hilo Hatties and strolled the block to historic Front Street.

This rugged town, which had once been the whaling mecca of the Hawaiian Islands, had transformed over the years to the tourist mecca of Maui. Both sides of the street were lined with art galleries, restaurants, boutiques, shirt shops, and souvenir stands selling everything from grass skirts to shark tooth necklaces.

Mary was still intent on finding a size forty-four double D coconut bra, but it seemed the shops catered to less formidable bosoms.

We passed several restaurants, but nothing seemed quite right until we reached the Lahaina Fish Company.

We peered into the restaurant and saw that the dining area was actually built out over the ocean, and we could hear the waves lapping the seawall under the tables.

"Oh, this looks perfect," Maggie whispered. "See if we can get a table by the rail."

Indeed we did, and just as we were seated, we were treated to a glorious sunset as the great orange ball quietly slid behind the silhouette of the island of Lanai across the channel.

From our vantage point along the rail, we had a perfect view of Lahaina Harbor. A massive cruise ship was anchored several hundred yards offshore, and busy tenders scurried between the ship and the dock carrying tourists and their wallets to eager shop owners. Another smaller, brightly decorated ship set a course parallel to the shore. Our server told us it was the *Lahaina Princess* making its regular evening sunset dinner cruise.

As darkness fell, a busboy lit tiki torches that extended from the restaurant out over the water, and their flickering flames danced on the swells breaking against the seawall beneath us.

Mary peered over the rail to the rocky seawall and exclaimed, "What are those ugly things crawling all over the rocks?"

We all took turns looking, and sure enough the rocks were alive with black crabs ranging in size from a half dollar to a saucer. As each wave struck the rocky shore, it appeared that the creatures would be washed away, but as the tide receded, they remained firmly attached.

After taking his turn, I heard Willie mutter, "I had de crabs once. Sho glad dey wasn't dat big and ugly."

That was probably more information than we needed just before dinner.

After a wonderful meal of *monchong*, *ono*, *opah*, and *mahi mahi*, we were full and sleepy and decided to call it a day because the next day another adventure awaited us.

The road to Hana.

Hana is a small village on the far southeast corner of the island. According to Liho, there's actually not much there. As the old saying goes, "It's not the destination but the journey."

The highway to Hana is fifty-two miles long and winds along Maui's eastern coast. What makes the trip so formidable is the fifty-nine one-lane bridges and 620 curves with tropical rainforests on one side and sheer cliffs sometimes dropping hundreds of feet to rocky shores below on the other.

Before the highway was widened into two lanes, just getting to Hana was a major feat. Shops sold T-shirts proudly declaring, "I survived the road to Hana!"

Today, if one is careful and you don't stop to gawk at each of the dozens of waterfalls, you can reach Hana in about three hours.

Liho picked us up, and we headed back across the island to Kahului. Our hotel was actually on the opposite side of the island from our destination.

It was going to be a long day.

The first little village we came to after leaving Kahului was Paia.

The eastern side of Maui faces the open ocean, and the trade winds come from that direction, so the surf is naturally bigger and rougher on that side. We had seen many regular surfers and kite surfers along the beach, and as we drove through Paia, Liho described the village as "hippie town," the hangout of choice for Maui's flower children and surfer dudes.

I probably wouldn't be spending much time there.

As we drove farther from the coastal plain and along the base of the great mountain, the green fields gradually transformed into tropical rainforest. The vegetation was so dense it was impossible to venture more that a few yards off the road.

We came to hairpin curves with old bridges dating from the 1930s spanning rocky streams carrying water from the summit of the mountain to the sea below. Waterfalls cascaded into icy pools surrounded by stalks of bamboo reaching fifty feet into the air.

Liho explained that since Maui had no rivers or underground reservoirs, the water supply for the entire island was dependent on the rain that fell in the forests on the mountainside.

Over one hundred thousand acres of the mountainside was under the control of the East Maui Irrigation System. Seventy-four miles of man-made ditches directed over four hundred and fifty million gallons of water per day to seven reservoirs.

This was my first exposure to a tropical rainforest, and the lush vegetation enthralled me. Green things of every size and description grew in abundance, from tiny ferns to huge elephant ears two feet across.

I made an offhand remark to no one in particular that I wished we had time to explore the forest, and to my surprise, Liho jumped on it right away.

"Hey, this is your vacation, and if you want to explore the forest, you should do it. We're not on a time schedule here. In fact, I know of a place coming up at the ten-mile marker I think you will enjoy. It's actually an access road for East Maui Irrigation. It runs from the highway up into the forest, and they use it to maintain the many miles of water ditches."

A few minutes later, Liho pulled to the side of the road next to a metal gate with a sign that read, "No Trespassing."

He saw me looking dubiously at the sign.

"Not to worry. They post signs like that everywhere, but people use this trail all the time. This is a favorite part of the forest for the local pig hunters."

"Pig hunters?"

"Oh yeah. These hills are full of feral pigs. The locals hunt them with dogs. The dogs corner a pig, and the hunters shoot them. Some guys still use knives and spears."

"And you're sure it's safe?"

"Absolutely. There is a bamboo forest about seventy-five yards up the trail. You'll love it. Just take your time, and I'll wait here by the car."

The four of us climbed through the gate, and after walking only a few dozen yards, it felt like we had entered the movie set of *One Million Years B.C.*

Huge trees with trunks three feet thick rose a hundred feet, and philodendron vines with leaves as big as your hand hung from the tallest branches. The humidity was so thick you could cut it with a knife, and tiny droplets of water hung on the tips of leafy ferns. A thick, green carpet of moss covered everything, and it seemed that at any moment some huge creature from that bygone era could come crashing through the forest.

After about fifty yards, the level trail became steep, and we huffed and puffed in the dense heat until we reached the towering bamboo.

Mary plopped down on a lava outcropping, and sweat dripped from every pore of her body.

"I can't go no farther." She wheezed. "I'm way too old for this shit. You all go ahead. I'm gonna stay right here and catch my breath then head back down to the car."

I looked at Maggie, expecting her to follow suit, but to my surprise, she cupped her hand behind her ear.

"Listen. Isn't that water rushing up ahead? Let's go take a look."

I looked at Willie.

"Hey, dis is cool and all, but I'se a city boy. Dis is way more woods dan I need. I'll stay wit Mary."

With that, our merry little band split up, and Maggie and I headed for the sound of the running water.

After another hundred yards, the trail leveled out, and we came to the source of the rushing water. It was one of the irrigation ditches, about two feet wide and three feet deep, and about a foot of water cascaded along to the waiting reservoir.

"Oh, look up there," Maggie squealed.

I looked in the direction she was pointing and saw that the irrigation ditch seemed to be cut right through the side of the mountain. The path followed along the edge of the ditch, and we marveled at the engineering required to build seventy-four miles of these amazing waterways.

We continued along the path, and each bend and turn brought new and exciting vistas of the lush forest.

Maggie grabbed my arm for the umpteenth time and pointed to a tall leafy plant about ten feet off the path.

"Is that what I think it is?" she said.

"Well, if you're thinking it's a banana tree, you're probably right."

We picked our way gingerly through the brush and stood staring at a stalk of bananas two feet long containing at least thirty pieces of the yellow fruit.

"Looks like they're ripe," I said, and I separated the two bottom bananas from the stem. "How cool is this? Here we are in the middle of a rainforest on a tropical island, eating bananas we found growing wild. Kind of like Robinson Crusoe."

"Or Tarzan and Jane." She snickered.

We walked another hundred yards, munching on our bananas, and came to a fork where another path intersected the one we were on.

We continued past that intersection, and in a short distance another path from a different direction intersected.

"Whoa, I think maybe we should turn back. We don't want to take the wrong turn on one of these paths and get lost up here. It might be days before anyone finds us."

"At least we wouldn't starve." She giggled.

We turned to retrace our steps and stopped short.

Two large Hawaiian men blocked our path.

I felt Maggie stiffen at my side.

We just stood there for the longest time, neither of us moving a muscle. I thought I heard footsteps behind me and turned to see two more Hawaiian men at our backs.

All four men walked to within a few feet of us.

I turned to the largest of the four. "Look, if we're not supposed to be here, I apologize. Our guide is at the bottom of the hill waiting for us. If it's okay, we'll just head back now."

I took a step to the side to go around him, and he blocked my way.

"Really," I said, "we don't want any trouble. We're just a couple of tourists enjoying your beautiful island. Again, if we've done something to offend you, I apologize."

I took another step, and he blocked my way again.

"You will come with us," was all he said.

I looked at Maggie and saw the terror in her eyes.

It took just a moment to assess our situation. There were four very strong Hawaiian guys and two of us. I was unarmed, and I noticed for the first time that two-foot machetes hung from their belts. We were surrounded by impenetrable forest. Our options were limited.

"Where are you taking us?"

"No questions. Now go!" He pointed down one of the intersecting paths.

"Walt, I'm scared," Maggie whispered.

"Yeah, me too. But I don't think we have much choice at this point. At least they haven't hurt us. Let's play along."

We walked for what seemed like hours through the dense jungle. We passed by waterfalls and crossed old bridges over bubbling streams.

Our captors never uttered a word. They just kept pushing us resolutely along the trail.

We came to a circular clearing hollowed out of the forest. Handmade log benches lined the perimeter, and wood was piled in a fire pit in the center of the ring.

Two wooden posts were set in the ground in front of the fire pit. A small thatched roof hut sat just outside the circle.

The tall man pushed us into the ring and pointed to the benches.

"Sit," he ordered.

We sat, and the men who had brought us stood to the side looking expectantly at the hut.

We heard rustling inside, and two men emerged.

One of them I had never seen before, but I recognized the other immediately.

Buddy Kalakoa!

"Well, well, if it isn't Walt Williams and Maggie McBride. Oh, wait. I guess it's Mr. and Mrs. Williams now. Congratulations."

I just sat there stunned.

"Buddy, what … ?" was all I could say.

"I'd like you to meet my father, Daniel Kalakoa."

"Buddy, what's this all about?"

"Oh, I think you know, Walter. We've had the conversation several times."

"Is this about the artifacts?"

"It's about more than just the artifacts, Walt. It's about Hawaiian independence. It's about taking back what is rightfully ours. It's about restoring the Hawaiian kingdom and going back to the old ways."

"But your family … your grandfather and uncle … "

"They were old fools. They sold out to the white man. They turned their backs on our heritage. They took the bones of our *alii* from their resting place and paraded them around for the world to see, and they paid for it with their lives."

"When they were killed, you were in charge of the exhibit. That's how the thieves knew back in Kansas City which trailer carried the artifacts and how they knew about the container on the barge."

"Can't put anything past you, can we, Walt?"

"So what now? What does this have to do with us? If you hadn't just told us, we would never have known about your involvement. Why now?"

"Uncle Ray may have been an old fool, but he also had a connection to the spirit world that has proven valuable to us."

"How so?"

"Do you remember the day in his office when he looked at your sweet bride and called her Hualani, the child of a chief?"

"So?"

"So the taking of the sacred artifacts angered the gods. They must be appeased. The artifacts must be returned to their proper place, and a sacrifice must be made. The only sacrifice that will satisfy the goddess Pele is one of royal blood. Hualani will be given to the goddess Pele."

I jumped to my feet and was immediately tackled by two of the Hawaiian guys.

"Bind them to the stakes," he ordered.

We were each grabbed by two men and taken to the stakes in the middle of the circle. Our hands and feet were bound, and we were left standing there side by side.

Maggie had not uttered a word since Buddy and his father had come out of the hut.

I turned to her.

"Maggie, I'm so sorry—"

"Stop. It's not your fault. How could you know that I am somehow related to a Hawaiian king? And whose idea was it to go to the gallery that day? If I didn't have free tickets, we never would have met Uncle Ray. I don't know why this is happening to us. All I want to do is be your wife and … and … "

She started sobbing.

It broke my heart to see her cry like that, and all I could do was stand there totally helpless.

She cried for a while and then became very quiet.

Finally, she said, "I love you, Walt."

"I love you too, Maggie. And somehow we're going to get out of this."

The Kalakoas retreated to their hut, leaving Maggie and me bound to the stakes under the watchful eyes of the burly Hawaiians.

Hours passed, and as darkness settled over the clearing, men and women began to emerge from the forest. At least twenty had gathered by the time Buddy and Daniel Kalakoa entered the ring.

"Light the ceremonial fire," he ordered. A man with a burning torch ignited the wood in the center of the ring. "Summon the great spirits," he ordered again, and another man lifted a conch shell to his lips.

As I listened to the blowing of the conch, it was hard to believe that just a few days ago I was filled with joy as Reverend Winslow summoned the good spirits to our wedding. Tonight, I was filled with dread.

Then Buddy spoke words in Hawaiian that I didn't understand, and two men began rhythmic tapping of a hollowed gourd.

Daniel Kalakoa strode to the middle of the circle and began to chant, and three women dressed in ti leaf skirts swayed to the plaintive words of the chant.

The chanting and dancing started slowly, but as the evening wore on, the ceremony rose to a feverish pitch.

Suddenly, Daniel raised his hands over his head, and the circle became deathly quiet.

He motioned to Buddy, who entered the ring with a small gourd in his hand. He stood in front of us with the gourd extended.

"It is time," he said. "You will drink."

"The hell I will," I replied.

He motioned to the tall Hawaiian who had brought us. He stood beside Maggie with one of those shark tooth war clubs.

"You will drink, or she will die before your eyes."

I looked at Maggie and whispered, "I love you."

Buddy put the gourd to my lips, and I swallowed the bitter liquid.

Everything turned black.

CHAPTER EIGHTEEN

I have only been under anesthetic once in my life when I had my wisdom teeth pulled, but I remember that when I awoke I was disoriented and confused.

When at last I stirred from the drug-induced sleep of Buddy's powerful potion, that same awful feeling overwhelmed me.

The last thing I remembered was standing in the ring and Buddy pressing the gourd to my lips, then nothing.

Gradually, my foggy brain began to clear, and I realized that I was shivering uncontrollably. I was totally surrounded by darkness except for a faint glow in the distance. I sat upright and explored the area around me with outstretched hands. The floor under me was solid rock, cold and hard, and I could hear wind whistling from the direction of the dim light.

I got to my knees and began to explore further when I touched something solid—it was Maggie!

My hand moved up her body, and I pressed my fingers to her neck, searching for a pulse. She was alive, but like me, her body was quivering with the biting cold. I pulled her body close to mine and shook her gently.

"Maggie! Maggie! Wake up!"

She moaned and stirred ever so slightly then went limp in my arms.

"Maggie! You've got to wake up!" I shook her again.

"Wha … where … Walt? Is that you?"

"Yes, I'm here. Can you hear me? Are you hurt?"

"Walt, I'm so cold. Where are we?"

"I'm not quite sure. Can you sit up?"

She struggled to a sitting position, and we just sat there, clinging to each other for warmth.

Little by little, our eyes grew accustomed to the dark, and I thought I could distinguish some objects a few feet from us. I started to move away from her to examine them more closely, but she held me tight.

"Please don't leave me. I'm so scared."

"Yeah, me too." I shivered. "But we can't just sit here. We'll freeze to death."

Reluctantly she loosened her grip, and I crawled over to the objects and began to explore them with my hands. I felt a gourd, then a wooden bowl, then some kind of mallet, and—oh, Lord—bones!

"Maggie, I know where we are. We're in one of those burial caves on the cliff face of the Haleakala Crater, and these are the artifacts from the exhibit."

I remembered something I had seen in the exhibit at the gallery.

"Stay right there. I've got to find something."

I crawled around the floor of the cave, my hands sweeping wide circles, and at last my fingers touched what I was looking for—the feathered cape.

I gathered it in my arms and whispered, "Maggie, where are you? Say something so I can find you."

"I'm over here."

I crawled to the sound of her voice, held her close, and wrapped our quivering bodies in the flowing feathered cape.

In time the feathers that had once protected their avian hosts provided the insulation we needed, and we huddled together against the biting cold.

In the relative comfort of our feathered tent, we began to take stock of our situation.

"Maggie, what happened after I passed out?"

"As soon as you were out, he made me drink that awful stuff too. The next thing I was aware of was you shaking me here in this cave."

"They must have transported us, along with the artifacts, back to the original burial site. They have said all along that the old bones should not have been disturbed, and now, according to them, they're back where they belong."

"I thought they were going to kill us."

"They probably thought they did. In the old days, when the volcano was active, human sacrifices were hurled into the bubbling caldron. Remember *Joe Versus the Volcano*? Anyway, now that the mountain is dormant, they probably figured that Haleakala would kill us by exposure to the elements. Either way, Pele would be appeased by the death of royalty."

"I understand that part, but why kill you?"

"Do you remember when Uncle Ray called me Kamamalu, the protector? I read somewhere that in the old days, when someone of royal blood died, those who served him in life were killed and buried with him to serve him in death. So I guess that's me."

"I'm so sorry I got you involved in this."

"Yeah, well, the least you could have done was warn me before we were married."

Just then, a bolt of lightning streaked across the sky, illuminating the entrance to the cave, and a clap of thunder seemed to shake the rock around us.

The whistling wind intensified, and in the distance we could hear rain pelting the floor of the cave.

"Since their goal was to kill us, I'm willing to bet that our hosts failed to stock this cave with Arbor Mist. If we're going to get out of this, we're going to need to drink. I found an old wooden bowl among the artifacts. I'm going to place it in the mouth of the cave to collect rainwater."

I left the warmth of the cape, found the wooden bowl, and scurried to the opening.

Cold and wet, I retreated to the comfort of my feathered princess, and we huddled together waiting for the cold, gray dawn.

The rain stopped as abruptly as it had come, and at last the opening became clearer as the first rays of light penetrated the cave.

"Shall we venture a look?" I suggested.

We moved to the mouth of the cave and cautiously peered over the edge.

The scene below took our breath away.

We were indeed in a cave on the sheer cliff face of Haleakala Crater. Hundreds of feet below, the massive cinder cones dotted the crater floor.

"How in the world did they get us in here?" Maggie asked.

I craned my neck upward. "We must have been low-ered from the top. It looks like we're maybe thirty feet below the rim."

"I'm sure glad I wasn't awake for that."

Just then, the rocks around us changed color as they reflected varying shades of crimson and gold.

We looked to our left just in time to see the morning sun burn through the clouds that hung low beneath the summit of the great mountain—sunrise on Haleakala.

As the sun rose in the sky, its rays fell upon the craggy peaks and cinder cones in the caldera, which in turn cast their eerie shadows on the crater floor.

It seemed that we were in another world as the ethereal shadow ballet unfolded before us.

"Oh, Walt, it's so beautiful."

We sat mesmerized, watching the shifting shadows as the sun continued its ascent into the heavens.

"The only thing that could make this more perfect is breakfast," I said. "Are you hungry?"

"Famished. Any ideas?"

"I thought the wife was supposed to fix breakfast. Isn't that in the wedding manual somewhere?"

"That's nothing but sexist propaganda. Anyway, I always thought guys were supposed to get the food when you're roughing it."

Then it occurred to me. I felt in my pocket, and sure enough, it was still there—a roll of Lifesavers that I had bought the day before at our junk food stop at the Pukalani Superette.

"Well, isn't this appropriate?" I said. "Lifesavers! And look, they're tropical fruit flavor." I peeled the wrapper away. "Would m'lady care for banana or papaya for breakfast?"

"Banana will do just fine."

So we sucked our Lifesavers and sipped our rainwater.

Like the old saying goes, "When life gives you lemons, make lemonade."

While our meager breakfast did little to nourish our bodies, it certainly lifted our spirits.

"Okay, Big Guy, how do we get out of here?"

"Well, we can't go up. It's a sheer climb of at least thirty feet to the top, so that only leaves down."

We peered over the lip of the cave, and twenty feet below, a rock ledge about eighteen inches wide jutted out from the cliff face. The ledge angled down to rocky outcroppings that could possibly provide hand- and footholds to the valley below.

A plan began to form in my mind. "If we could only make it to that ledge, we might have a chance."

"That's a pretty big *if.*"

"Where's Spiderman when you need him?"

"And what if we get to the crater floor? What then?"

"Do you remember the map in the visitor's center?"

"Yes."

I pointed to the crater wall across the valley. "See that V in the valley wall? That's Kaupo Gap, and there's a trail that leads through the gap to the other side of the island. If I remember correctly, there are even some primitive cabins somewhere along the trail."

"So your great plan is to jump down to that ledge, climb hundreds of feet down the cliff face, and hike across the crater floor through the gap to the other side of the island?"

"In a nutshell."

"Are you crazy? We're sixty-seven years old. The most strenuous thing we have done recently is the dance contest at the Class Reunion Lounge."

"Well, we can't stay here. Those guys could come back at any time to make sure their sacrifice worked. Do you have any better ideas?"

She thought for a minute. "No."

"I didn't think so."

I looked over the lip to the rock ledge twenty feet below. It might as well have been a hundred feet. We just couldn't reach it.

I leaned back against the rock wall of the cave and was pondering our impossible situation, when a tiny gecko popped up over the edge to bask in the morning sunlight.

He stared at me, and I stared at him. Then I remembered Uncle Ray's words as he handed me the little obsidian lizard: "Take *mo'o'ala*. He is your *aumakua*. He will guide you."

"Well," I said, "if you have any suggestions, this would be a good time."

To my surprise, he scurried across the floor of the cave into the dark recesses where the artifacts rested.

On an impulse, I hopped to my feet and followed him.

I noticed for the first time that the artifacts were in a kind of lean-to fashioned of bamboo poles. The roof was composed of the broad leaves of some tropical plant. The little lizard had climbed the lean-to and was sitting on a heavy cord that bound the bamboo poles together.

Our eyes met again, and he scurried off into the darkness.

Maggie had witnessed this improbable scenario and followed me into the cave. We stood side-by-side staring at the lashings that could be our ticket out of the cave.

"This is just too weird," she whispered.

"Yeah, but it just might work."

We began removing the leafy fronds from the framework and untying the lashings that held the poles together. When everything was disassembled, we tied the lashings together to form a long rope.

"Do you think this will hold us?" she asked.

"Only one way to find out."

I draped the rope over a rock that protruded from the wall and hung suspended off the floor. It was amazingly strong.

We carried the rope to the lip of the cave and dropped one end over the edge. To our dismay, it was about four feet too short.

"So near and yet so far," she muttered.

I made a closer examination of the rope. It had been woven from the fibers of some kind of plant.

Then an idea struck me.

I hurried back into the cave and brought back some of the large fronds that had covered the roof of the structure. They looked a lot like the material of which the rope was made. Maggie looked on as I began to tear the huge leaves into strips.

"Do you know how to braid?" I asked.

"Does a bear crap in the woods?"

You've gotta love her spunk.

I tore strips, and Maggie braided. Before long we had another six feet of rope to attach to our escape ladder.

"Now all we need is a sky hook," I quipped. "Any ideas what we're going to tie this thing to?"

She thought for a minute and hurried back into the cave. She returned with one of the long bamboo poles from the lean-to.

It was just long enough to wedge between the sides of the cave opening.

We tied one end to the pole and threw the other over the side. The end dangled just a few inches from the floor of the ledge.

"Okay, now comes the fun part," I said. "I'm going to go first. If the rope will hold my weight, it will certainly hold yours. Then I'll hopefully be on the ledge to help you down."

This was the moment of truth. If this didn't work, I would be lying in a bloody heap hundreds of feet below, and Maggie would be left to die a long and painful death from exposure.

We held each other close, knowing that this could be our last embrace.

Finally I broke away and said with a bravado that I didn't actually feel, "We're going to be okay. I'm not nearly through being your husband."

She smiled a weak smile. "Be careful. I love you."

I gripped the bamboo pole and slid my belly over the edge until I bent at the waist and my feet dangled in midair.

I made the mistake of looking down. The ledge wasn't actually that far below, but the distance to the crater floor made my head swim. I wrapped the vine rope around my leg, said a silent prayer, and slid off the ledge.

The rope held, and slowly I inched my way down to the ledge. I cannot describe the relief I felt when my feet finally touched the rock outcropping.

I looked up and gave Maggie a big thumbs-up. "Your turn. It's not too bad. Just don't look down."

Maggie slid over the edge as she had seen me do and wrapped her leg around the rope. I steadied the rope on my end, and she began her descent. It took just a few moments for her to reach me, but it seemed like an eternity. When at last she was by my side, I held her close until we both stopped shaking.

"It'll be a walk in the park from here," I said.

Then I looked at what lay ahead.

The rock ledge angled down and to our left and, to my dismay, narrowed to about six inches, where it ended in another outcropping.

I inched my way along the ledge and saw that on the other side of the rock, indentions in the cliff face would suffice as hand and footholds. I motioned for Maggie to follow me. Gingerly, I hugged the rock and slid around to the first foothold.

"Watch where I step, and if I don't go crashing down the mountain, follow me."

"You inspire such confidence," she replied.

Each step was a crap-shoot. I held on for dear life as I placed my weight on each rocky outcrop. Some held, and some gave way under my weight, sending an avalanche of debris cascading to the crater floor.

The weather was an uncomfortable paradox. The temperature couldn't have been more than the high fifties, but in the thin atmosphere I could feel the sun's rays penetrating my exposed flesh.

Luckily, every fifty feet or so, there would be a ledge wide enough to hold us both and provide a brief respite from our arduous descent.

The sun was high in the sky when we finally reached the crater floor. We looked back and up, and the opening into the cave appeared no bigger than a pinhead. It felt so good to be standing on level, solid ground.

"Well, so far, so good," Maggie said. "At least we're still in one piece."

"Not too bad for a couple of old farts," I replied. "The rest should be a piece of cake."

I had to quit saying that.

While the trek across the crater floor was certainly not as dangerous as the first leg of our journey, it was no less taxing.

Instead of dirt, the floor was composed of tiny grains of volcanic debris that shifted and gave way under our weight—literally, the old two steps forward and one step back.

We soon discovered why it was called "Sliding Sands."

Doggedly, we trudged in the direction of the V and passed through the gap just as the sun was slipping below the western rim of the crater.

"It can't be too much farther to the first cabin," I said. "We really need to get there before dark."

Maggie was totally exhausted, but the idea of spending another night exposed to the elements created a sense of urgency, and we pressed on. Night was about to overtake us when we saw the small wood cabin in the clearing ahead.

The door was unlocked, and we stepped into one large room with two beds consisting of a frame and metal springs and a small cabinet.

There was, of course, no electricity or sanitary facilities. There was a spigot, but the sign above it read, "Water is not potable."

Swell!

"It certainly isn't the Motel Six," I said.

"Walt, you take me to the nicest places for our honeymoon."

At least she hadn't lost her sense of humor.

I looked around outside and saw a stack of firewood and kindling.

"Okay, Boy Scout," Maggie said, "let's see you rub two sticks together and get this thing going."

"I don't know about sticks, but I can think of something I'd like to rub together to get some heat going."

"In your dreams, Buster."

You can't blame a guy for trying.

We found two matches in the wooden cabinet. I gathered dry leaves and tiny twigs and built a little teepee. We held our breath as I struck the first match and held it to the tinder.

The tinder smoked, and with a few well-placed breaths, a tiny flame ignited. The twigs caught, and soon we were sitting beside a roaring fire.

It's absolutely amazing that when all the trappings of modern society are stripped away and you are left with just the basic elements needed to sustain life, if you are with the one you love, it is enough.

We sat in the light of the campfire, and I pulled the roll of Lifesavers from my pocket. "Mango or coconut?" I asked. "Oh, wait. I'll take the first one. It's covered with pocket lint."

We sucked on our supper wishing we had something tall and cold to drink, and soon, it was as if some genie had granted our wish.

The lightning flashed, thunder rolled, and rain fell in torrents.

We made a dash for the cabin, and I placed an old tin cup on the step to catch the precious liquid.

I would have guessed that the bare springs of the old bed would be unbearably uncomfortable, but we were so exhausted and spent that we were out like a light the minute we lay down together.

When we awoke, the sun was pouring in the window of the cabin. I tried to move, but my old body said, "No!" I felt like I had been run over by a semi, but at least we were alive.

We pried our aching bodies off the cot, ate our last two Lifesavers, and drank deeply of the precious rainwater. We started down the trail that would eventually take us to the coastal highway.

As the trail descended, the vegetation became more lush, and soon we were surrounded by a forest not unlike the one from which we had been taken. To Maggie's delight, we found another stalk of ripe bananas and wolfed down two each.

We had just rounded a bend in the trail when we came face to face with a huge hound. He seemed to be as surprised as we were, and we just stood there looking at each other.

He bared his teeth and started advancing toward us with a low growl.

"Don't move a muscle," I whispered.

The dog would advance a few steps and stop and then advance a few more steps. He was about fifteen feet from us when two Hawaiian men bearing rifles came into view. The first one gave a command in Hawaiian, and the big dog sat back on his haunches.

I remembered what Liho had said, so I thought I would give it a try.

"You guys hunting pigs?"

He thought for a minute. "Ugh, yes, pigs."

He looked first at me and then even longer at Maggie, and then he turned to his companion. They spoke to each other in Hawaiian.

He turned back to me and said, "The Old One said you would be coming. You will come with us."

Oh no, not again, I thought.

When we didn't move, he spoke again, "You are Hualani, and we must take you to the Old One. You will be safe."

I looked at Maggie. "We've come this far. Let's see how it plays out."

We followed the men down the trail to an old jeep. He motioned for us to get in the back, and the old dog jumped in after us. He stuck his snout in my crotch, sniffed, and, seemingly satisfied, laid his head in my lap.

I wasn't about to argue.

We drove down the mountain to the coastal high-way, turned left, and drove through the little village of Hana.

After about an hour, we turned off the main high-way onto a side road. The sign said, "*Nahiku*," and the road seemed to descend slowly to the rocky coast below.

We pulled off the paved road and followed a gravel road several hundred yards back through the jungle. We came to a small house in a clearing. The jeep came to a halt, and we were directed toward the cottage.

The door swung open, and to my surprise, out stepped—Nathan!

CHAPTER NINETEEN

"Welcome, friends," he said. "I thought we would be seeing each other again. Come in. You must be starving and dry as a bone. Here, sit. I'll get you something to eat and drink."

I stared in amazement. In my wildest dreams I would never have guessed that I would ever see again the old man whose bicycle I had stolen.

In a few moments, he returned with pulled pork, fruit, and tall glasses of ice water. We ravenously attacked the meal provided by our host. Nothing so simple had ever tasted so good.

After the food had taken the edge off of our hunger, I turned to Nathan. "The men who brought us here said you knew we would be coming. How?"

"It's very simple, Walter. Raymond and Ronald Kalakoa were good friends of mine. He called me after your visit to the art gallery. I will miss them very much."

"Then I guess you know that they were killed by Buddy and Daniel Kalakoa."

"Such a tragedy. The ideologies that divide my people, that divide families, are not unlike your Civil War."

"This is all about sovereignty, isn't it? The restoration of the old Hawaiian kingdom?"

"Yes, that and more. There are those who believe that the lands taken from our people should be returned as well."

"Since we're sitting here enjoying your hospitality, would it be safe to assume that your sympathies lie with Uncle Ray?"

"I am sympathetic to both sides, but I am also a pragmatist. I totally understand the loss felt by those seeking sovereignty, but I also know the chances that our land will be returned are about as great as the island of Manhattan being returned to the Indians.

"Do I wish that things could have been different? Absolutely! But as the old saying goes, 'You can't unring a bell.'

"The majority of the kanaka believe as Uncle Ray, his brother, and I believe. It is what it is, and we can't change it. So we must make the best of what we have. We must educate our children and pass on the history of our culture. Artifacts of our ancestors should be proudly displayed to tell our story to the world, not hidden to wither away into dust."

"And what of the return to the 'old ways'? Maggie and I were to be sacrificed to appease the goddess Pele, who was angered by the removal of the artifacts."

"Gods do not get angry. Men get angry, and they justify their acts of aggression by creating gods and bestowing them with human emotions."

"I can see how that might apply to the gods of the early Polynesians, but I noticed when you were preaching on Front Street that you were quoting the Bible. Isn't the God depicted there angry and vengeful?"

"Indeed he is, and it's really no different. You see, there's an order to things in nature. Some years there is drought; some years there are floods; some years insects overrun crops, and so it goes. Why do these things happen? Even today with all our knowledge, we cannot predict or alter that which nature brings.

"Imagine the early Polynesians or the early Hebrews. For lack of understanding or a better explanation, a crop failure must be the work of a powerful supreme being who is angered."

"So are you saying that you don't believe in a higher power?"

"Not at all. Just look around you, from the tiniest creature to the vastness of the universe above. It is amazing to me that there are those who believe that all we see came to be by accident alone. But again, because of our lack of understanding, we have limited our vision of creation to that which we know.

"I do not believe that the demi-god Maui pulled the Hawaiian Islands from the ocean floor, nor do I believe that all that is in the heaven and earth was created in seven days."

"And what about the return to the old *kapu* social order?"

"Every society has rules that must be followed if it is to survive. When my ancestors settled these islands, they soon discovered that there were certain things that should be done and certain things that must not be done, and the survival of the entire population depended on everyone following the rules. Their very existence was so precarious that violators were put to death.

"Is that so different from the Ten Commandments that Moses brought to his people? The difference being that the punishment for breaking those rules was a spiritual death.

"But all that was for a different day and time. Today, we also have commandments that must be adhered to if we are to live together peacefully. There are laws to be followed and punishment for those who break them."

"Okay, one last question. How does this fit into the scheme of things?" I pulled the little obsidian lizard out of my pocket.

"Ah, *mo'o'ala*, your *aumakua*. Has he been helpful to you?"

"Well, yeah. Actually he...I guess the first time...then later...and when we were in the cave..."

"Hard to explain, isn't it? Walter, I am just an old man, and I don't have all the answers. All I know is that there are forces in nature beyond our understanding, and wise is the man that quietly listens to the promptings of that which is more powerful than himself."

Maggie had been sitting quietly listening to Nathan and me trying to solve the mysteries of the universe. Tiring of our musings, she brought our immediate situation into focus.

"Okay, guys, that's all well and good, but we were just kidnapped by political zealots, drugged, and left to die in a cave inside a volcano. Where do we go from here?"

"Ah, my dear. I am just an old windbag. Such matters are better left to the experts."

Just then there was a knock at the door, and Detective Harry Chinn entered the room.

"Well, well, Walt and Maggie. I understand that you two have had quite an adventure."

"Harry, how did you know—"

"My wife is Nathan's niece. He keeps me in the loop. Why don't you start from the beginning at the gallery in Kansas City and tell me everything that's happened up till now."

Maggie and I shared all that we knew about the artifacts, the murders, and our abduction and escape. When we had finished, our story sounded unbelievable even to us.

"We figured from the beginning that all of this was the work of the sovereignty group," Harry said, "but we just didn't have any hard evidence to link them to any specific act, until now. They assumed that their admission to you would be safe. After all, you'd soon be dead."

"So what now?" I asked.

"I know you want to get back to the hotel and your friends and continue your honeymoon, but we need to stop at the station in Kahului to take your statement. As soon as that is on paper, we'll have enough to arrest the Kalakoas. If they go back to the cave and find you missing, they just might bolt."

"Our friends!" I shouted. "What happened to Willie and Mary after our abduction? I was so wrapped up in our mess that I completely forgot about them. They must be going crazy."

"When you didn't return from your little hike, Liho called and reported you missing. We immediately sent out a search party, but, of course, you had been taken from the area. Liho drove your friends back to the hotel. They were understandably upset. I had to threaten to lock up your friend Mary. She was insisting that they be allowed to join the search party. That's all we needed was two more tourists roaming around in the rainforest. She finally gave in.

"We've had Liho keeping an eye on them. When Nathan notified us of your arrival, we let them know you are safe."

We thanked Nathan for his hospitality and headed to Kahului to give our statements. That being done, Detective Chinn assigned an officer to drive us back across the island to our hotel. His final words as we drove away were, "Thanks to you both. By the time you are back to your hotel, the Kalakoas will be under arrest."

Weary and worn, we headed to our room, but we stopped on the way to see Willie and Mary. We knocked, but there was no answer.

"Must be on the beach," I muttered. We walked across the path and looked in both directions, but no Willie and Mary.

"Let's try by the pool," Maggie suggested.

We trudged back to the pool and then looked around the tiki bar, but our friends were nowhere to be seen. Deciding they must have gone to Lahaina to shop, we returned to our room for a hot shower and a well deserved rest.

Just as we opened the door, the phone rang.

"Walt, this is Harry. They have Willie and Mary."

CHAPTER TWENTY

"What are you talking about?" I asked. "Who has them?"

"The Kalakoas. Somehow they learned of your escape and probably figured that with your testimony the jig was up. It would only be a matter of time until the cops came calling. But the puzzler is why did they snatch your friends instead of making a run for it?"

"So what about Willie and Mary? Did they tell you where they're holding them?"

"Nope. They won't tell us a thing right now. But here's the weird part: they say they'll cop to everything but they have to talk to Hualani first. They're insisting that they must talk to Maggie."

"Not a chance! I don't want Maggie anywhere close to those crazy bastards."

"Well, it's your call, but it may be the only way we can locate your friends."

"Let me talk to Maggie, and I'll call you back."

Maggie sat and listened dumbfounded.

"I just don't get this whole 'Hualani' thing. It nearly got us killed, and now our friends are in danger. We can't just go to bed and do nothing. I don't want to see those guys any more than you do, but we've got to put an end to this. Let's shower and clean up and get it over with."

I called Detective Chinn and told him to send a car for us.

As my grandmother used to say, "There's no rest for the weary."

Harry met us at the station and led us to an interview room where the Kalakoas were being held under guard. We all found seats around the table, and Harry turned to the Kalakoas. "Okay, you got what you wanted. Now spill it."

Daniel just sat quietly, looking at both of us, then finally spoke. "We underestimated you, Hualani, and your Kamamalu. We should have known that one that carries the blood of an *alii* would be a worthy adversary."

"Cut the crap, Daniel," Maggie retorted. "I'm really tired of all this 'Hualani' business. I'm not a princess or royalty. I'm just an ordinary woman who's sick of your bullshit! Now where are our friends?"

Daniel just smiled condescendingly. "You are who you are, and nothing can change that. You have a destiny to fulfill, and you will do so with our help."

"It doesn't look like you're in any position to make demands," Harry interjected.

"Ah, but you're forgetting about their friends. If they want to see them again, you will all cooperate. We too have a destiny to fulfill. When we learned of your escape, we knew that their safe return would ensure your full cooperation."

I turned to Buddy. "How can you do this? After all we've been through. And to murder your grandfather and uncle—what could be so important to warrant all of this?"

"I would not expect you to understand," he replied. "My people have had *everything* taken from them—their land, their form of government, their religion, and their self-respect. We do what we do to honor our ancestors and to restore the Hawaiian kingdom to its former greatness. Our cause is greater than family or friends, and no one must stand in our way.

"You have never lived where your homeland has been taken over by strangers from across the sea that impose their laws and ways on your people. Until you have lived it, you will never understand it."

"So the ends justify the means, no matter what the cost?"

"In revolution, there is sacrifice. There is a price to pay for the greater good."

"You asked for our cooperation for the safe return of our friends. What is it you want?"

"My father and his brother foolishly removed the bones of our *alii* from their resting place and angered the gods," Daniel said. "They paid with their lives, but Pele will only be appeased with the blood of royalty. Hualani must offer a blood sacrifice to save her friends."

This was just too much, and I reached across the table and grabbed Daniel by the throat. Harry was on me in a flash and pulled me back into my chair.

A startled but smiling Daniel rubbed his neck. "So my American friend has passion too. Such a rash act. Did the end justify the means?"

I had played right into his hands.

"You reacted too soon, my friend," Daniel continued. "You did not let me explain. We are not asking for Hualani to give her life, just some blood and a lock of her hair. We will take these to the cave and offer a sacrifice to Pele. Then we will release your friends."

Harry jumped to his feet. "If you think we're going to let you go, you're out of your mind."

"Of course not. You will take us there in your custody, we will offer our sacrifice, and our work will be done. There are others to carry on our cause."

"So if Maggie is willing to part with some blood and a lock of hair and Harry is willing to take you to the cave, you will make your offering, remain in custody, and tell us where you're holding Willie and Mary? Is that the deal?"

"That is the deal."

"And if we refuse?"

"Your friends mean nothing to us. There are places in the rainforest that no man has ever seen."

I looked at Maggie and Harry.

Maggie spoke first. "Hey, if all it takes is a lock of hair and a pint of blood to get our friends back, I'm in."

Harry was more reluctant. "I don't like making deals with criminals, especially with zealots. There's got to be more to it than this. They're not telling us everything."

"You will be in control all the way," Daniel said. "We both get what we want. We shall fulfill our destiny, and you will get your friends back."

Harry grudgingly acquiesced. "Okay, but we do it my way. I'll order a chopper that will fly us to the crater rim. We'll access the cave from a rope ladder and wait while you perform your ceremony; then it's back to jail for the both of you. Understand?"

"Agreed."

Harry arranged for the chopper, and Maggie had blood drawn by an EMT.

There was only enough room in the chopper for four passengers and the pilot, so Maggie stayed behind at the precinct. The Kalakoas, cuffed and shackled, carrying their blood offering, boarded the chopper with Harry and me, and we lifted off to climb to the summit of the great volcano.

Fortunately, it was a clear day. The clouds that so often hid Haleakala's summit were absent, and our destination was clearly visible ten thousand feet above the valley floor.

I had only seen the cave opening from the floor of the crater and had no idea how to locate it from the crater's rim, but Buddy directed the pilot, and soon we were hovering outside the cave opening in the sheer cliff wall.

Looking at the gaping hole brought back vivid memories of the ordeal Maggie and I had endured, and as I looked at the rocky cliff face we had climbed down, I silently uttered a prayer of thanks.

I recognized the cave immediately, but something in my mind registered as not being quite right. I couldn't put my finger on it.

It was impossible to get the whirring blades close enough to the wall to access the opening directly, so the chopper lifted the thirty feet to the crater's rim. We dropped a rope ladder to the cave mouth below.

Thankfully, the thirty-five-mile-an-hour winds that often buffeted the summit were calm. Dangling from a thirty-foot rope ladder wildly swaying in the breeze was not my idea of a good time.

Harry descended first so that he could help our shackled prisoners off the ladder, and I was last, carrying the blood and lock of hair in a bag slung over my shoulder. When we were all safely inside, I handed the bag to Daniel.

The artifacts were located at the back of the cave, maybe fifty feet from the opening, to protect them from the elements. I had told Harry that to my knowledge the opening in the cliff wall was the only way in and out, so we waited by the mouth while the Kalakoas made their way into the depths of the cave.

While we waited, the uneasy feeling that I had continued to plague me.

Then it came to me. I knew what was wrong.

When Maggie and I climbed down to the ledge, the vine rope was attached to a bamboo pole wedged between the walls of the cave opening.

The pole and rope were missing. Someone had been to the cave after we escaped.

I whispered to Harry, "This is all wrong. Someone's been here. They could have left guns or anything back in that cave. I think we've walked into a trap."

"Oh crap! Are you sure?"

"Absolutely!"

Harry pulled his service revolver just as the Kalakoas emerged from the darkness. But they were not carrying guns as I feared. They were carrying two packages, each about the size of a brick, wrapped in duct tape.

Harry pointed his weapon. "Okay, whatever you've got there, just put it on the ground."

"I don't think so, Harry," Daniel said, "and I wouldn't think about shooting, because if I release my grip on this trigger, this C-4 will blow you all to hell."

Harry holstered his gun. "Okay, take it easy. So what now? You don't think you're going to get on the chopper with that stuff, do you?"

"Absolutely not. We came to fulfill our destiny, and that's what we're going to do. After today, the bones of our forefathers will never be disturbed again. They will rest in peace, and Pele will be appeased. Our work will be finished."

"What about our friends?" I said. "Where are Willie and Mary?"

"I'm sure my comrades will find a way to make good use of them. They are merely a tool, a means to an end, as you might say."

"But we had a deal!"

"Your friend Harry was right. You should never make deals with 'criminals' or 'zealots.'" Daniel placed a package of the explosive against the wall on each side of the cave entrance. "You have about ten seconds to make your exit. Farewell."

Daniel and Buddy turned and walked back into the dark reaches of the cave.

"Walt, run!" Harry shouted. "Let's get the hell out of here."

I didn't need a second invitation.

The rope ladder was still dangling just outside the cave entrance, suspended from the hovering chopper. I grabbed the ladder and began scrambling up, hand over fist. Harry was right behind me. The minute he was on the ladder, he shouted to the pilot, "Up! Get us up! *Fast!*"

The pilot gunned the engine, and we were lifted skyward hanging from the end of the swinging rope ladder.

"Hang on tight, Walt! We're gonna get hit!"

The C-4 exploded with all the fury of Pele herself.

My first sensation was the deafening roar that assaulted my eardrums, causing me to cringe in pain. Following close on the heels of the thunder came the concussion wave from the explosion.

In movies, I had seen people fleeing from a blast that were lifted off their feet and thrown through the air, and I always wondered if that was real or just Hollywood.

It was real.

The wave hit us with a force that took my breath away. The chopper was battered like a gnat in a stiff wind, and our rope ladder, which had been hanging vertically, was lifted ninety degrees to a horizontal position. It was all we could do hang on in the turbulent air.

Next came the rocks and debris that were propelled from the blast site like double-aught buckshot from a twelve gauge. We did our best to protect our eyes and face, but our bodies took the brunt of the bruising rocks.

It was over as quickly as it had come.

As soon as the chopper leveled out and the rope ladder stabilized, we climbed to safety.

The pilot made a pass by the spot where the cave opening used to be. All that remained was a mound of rubble belching plumes of dust.

Daniel and Buddy Kalakoa had fulfilled their destiny and sealed their own fate by sealing off from the world the remains of their beloved ancestors.

Their comrades would hold them up as martyrs, their death breathing new life into the sovereignty movement.

But also dying with them was any hope of finding my friends alive.

CHAPTER TWENTY-ONE

s the chopper swooped down from the summit, I saw a huge black mushroom cloud rising hundreds of feet into the air from the base of the mountain just below Pukalani.

I turned to Harry and pointed to the cloud. "I thought you said this volcano was dormant. If that's not an eruption, then Japan must be bombing us again."

Harry just smiled. "It's nothing quite as dramatic as all that. It's just a sugarcane burn. When the cane is ready to harvest, they burn the fields to eliminate the weeds and the leaves from the stalk."

"But doesn't that burn the cane stalks too?"

"No, the cane stalk is eighty-five percent liquid, and the field burns so fast that the stalk is left intact. A forty-acre field, like the one you see below, will completely burn in fifteen to twenty minutes. They use dozers to clear a twenty-foot area around the field so that the fire is contained."

From our vantage point high above the field, I saw the billowing black smoke rise high into the air, and as it drifted west in the prevailing trade winds, the black turned into a dirty gray.

"That's our 'Maui snow,'" Harry said. "It drifts into Kihei and settles on the lanais and cars and really pisses off the *haoles* who paid a half million for their condo in paradise."

"We all have our crosses to bear," I said.

Harry just smiled.

On the ride from the heliport to the station, I kept playing the events of the past few days over in my mind, and something just didn't add up.

We found Maggie waiting anxiously in the conference room at the precinct. She was visibly shaken after hearing of our harrowing escape and the death of the Kalakoas. And worst of all, we were no closer to finding our missing friends.

"I've been thinking about how all of this played out," I said, "and something smells really fishy. Help me think this through.

"We were on the road to Hana, and I said something like, 'I'd like to explore the jungle,' and Liho dropped us off at the East Maui Irrigation Trail. We hadn't been on the trail more than fifteen or twenty minutes when those guys nabbed us. How did they know we were there? We must have passed a dozen trails leading from the highway into the forest. Why did he pick that one?"

"Unless it was prearranged," Harry said. "Even if you hadn't said anything, he may have stopped there anyway. Your statement just made the stop seem more reasonable."

"Now think about this," I continued. "Who knew we had escaped from the cave? If I understood correctly, Nathan called you to tell you we were safe at his place. When you arrived, you told us that after we went missing, Willie and Mary returned to the hotel, and you asked Liho to keep an eye on them. Is that right?"

"Right on, so far."

"Then you told us that as soon as you heard we were safe, you relayed the information to Willie and Mary so they wouldn't worry. Who did you call?"

"Liho!"

"By the time we returned to the hotel, they had been kidnapped, so someone who knew we had escaped tipped off the Kalakoas, who nabbed our friends to use as bargaining chips to get us all back to the cave. So who knew that we had escaped and the location of Willie and Mary?"

"Liho!"

Then a terrible thought occurred to me. *They don't need them for bargaining chips anymore. They are expendable.*

"I think it's time we paid a visit to your old friend and guide, Liho," Harry said.

"He dances at the hotel every evening," I said. "He'll probably be there by the time we drive across the island."

"Then let's get moving."

We stopped at the front desk and asked the concierge if she had seen Liho. She told us that he was in the dressing room behind the stage by the tiki bar.

The dressing room was small, maybe six feet wide and twelve feet long, and the walls were lined with costumes, gourds, and drums. Liho was in the process of selecting his wardrobe for the evening's performance when we entered.

Harry didn't waste any time.

"Liho, we need to talk, and I think you know why."

Liho looked at each of us and hung his head. I saw his shoulders slump, and his huge body quivered with emotion as he fought back the tears.

"I ... I ... I didn't want to do it," he stammered. "I'm not a part of their movement. But they brought me this." He pulled a photograph of a woman and small boy from his pocket.

"This is my sister and her son, my nephew. They live on Oahu. Buddy Kalakoa told me that if I didn't cooperate, his 'friends' from Waimanolo would pay her a visit and it wouldn't be pleasant."

"Why didn't you come to us for help?" Harry asked.

"How do you know who to trust these days? Anyone could be part of their movement—even you or one of your men. And if they find out I have talked, my sister will pay the price." He turned to Maggie and me. "I'm so sorry. I know you trusted me, and I let you down, but I just didn't know what else to do."

"I understand, Liho," I said. "We've all been caught up in this thing, but we've got another problem right now. I suppose you know that they took Willie and Mary."

"Yes, the men came to their room and knocked, and they opened right away hoping it was the two of you returning. They took them at gunpoint. I saw them being shoved in a van, and they drove away."

"Do you have any idea where they might have taken them?" Harry asked.

"I recognized one of the men. He has a place out by Kahakuloa. That would be my guess."

"Kahaku—what?" I asked. "Where's that?"

"Kahakuloa," Harry replied. He pointed toward the mountains behind us. "It's on the coast on the other side of these mountains."

"Then let's get rolling," I said.

"Not a chance. First, it's not a place you want to go. After you pass Honokohou Bay, the road narrows to one lane. There are sheer cliffs on the mountain side and vertical drops to the rocky coast below on the ocean side. There is only room for one car, and if you meet someone coming from the other direction, one of you has to drive backwards to a wide spot cut into the mountain. Second, you two have been through enough. You need to get some rest. This is your honeymoon, after all."

"But they're our friends and—"

"And nothing. Let us do our job. We'll find your friends."

"And what about me?" Liho said. "Am I under arrest?"

Harry looked at Maggie and me. "Do you want to press charges?"

"I expect that if I was in Liho's shoes and it was Maggie they were threatening, I would have done the same thing. I think we'll pass on the charges."

Liho grabbed my hand and thanked me, but I thought it odd that he wouldn't look me in the eye.

As we turned to leave, Noelani entered the dressing room. Seeing us about to leave, she stepped back to give us room to exit the tiny space.

As I passed by her, I felt her slip a piece of paper into my hand. I started to speak, but a quick shake of her head and the look in her eye told me to keep moving.

Back in the privacy of our room, I unfolded the note.

It read, "Meet me by the scuba shack after our performance. Your friends are in danger."

We showered, put on fresh clothing, and headed back to the tiki bar for supper. We ordered fish sandwiches and fries and enjoyed our supper while Liho, Noelani, and the trio onstage performed their evening hula show. At the conclusion of the show, the dancers retreated to the dressing room to change out of their costumes. Liho left first, and a few minutes later we saw Noelani leave and walk in the direction of the beach. We waited a few minutes so that anyone watching would not suspect that we were following her.

The beach was pretty much deserted at that time of the evening. As we approached the shack, Noelani called to us from the shadows. "I'm here."

"What's this all about? Why the secrecy?"

"I was behind the dressing room when you were talking to Liho. It was none of my business, but the walls are very thin, and I heard your conversation. The police aren't going to find your friends at Kahakuloa."

"How do you know that?"

"Because I saw two men talking to Liho earlier, before you and the policeman arrived. I sort of heard some of that conversation too."

"You seem to have a knack for that. What did you hear?"

"They told Liho that the Kalakoas were dead and that it would be just a matter of time until you put two and two together and figured out that he was part of the plan. They knew you would be coming to confront Liho, so they told him to send the cops to Kahakuloa to throw them off."

"So all that was just a wild goose chase?"

"I'm afraid so."

"So Liho double-crossed us again?"

"Not really. He truly wants no part of this, but they threatened his sister again. He felt he had no choice."

"No wonder he wouldn't look me in the eye."

"Liho's a good man, but he's caught between a rock and a hard place."

"So Willie and Mary are not at Kahakuloa. Do you have any idea where they might be holding them?"

"I don't know for certain, but I did recognize one of the men. He is a watchman at the Kaheawa wind farm."

"The what?"

"Do you remember seeing the huge windmills on the mountain above McGregor Point?"

"Yes."

"That's the wind farm. It's very isolated, and there's a maintenance shed on site. It would be a perfect place to stash your friends."

"So how do we get there?"

"There's a service road right by McGregor Point that goes directly to the wind farm, but they keep the gate locked, and sometimes there's a guard there. There are two other ways to the farm. Just past the tunnel through the mountain on the way to Lahaina is the entrance to the Lahaina Pali Trail. Before the highway was built, the only way to get to Lahaina from Kahului was across the mountain by foot or on horseback. That trail crosses the wind farm service road. There are signs there that warn hikers to stay off the service road, but lots of curious tourists wander up there. That could be your diversion."

"Diversion from what?"

"From you coming up to the wind farm from the backside. Where the Pali Trail comes down the mountain by Maalaea, there is another trail that goes directly up the mountain. It is actually a service road for the power lines that bring electric service to west Maui. Not many people know about it, and few would want to hike it if they did know."

"Why is that?"

"While the Pali Trail has a few steep spots, it's fairly easy to hike because the rise is gradual. The power line trail is straight up the mountain, and it's a three-thousand-foot climb to the back of the wind farm."

"So what you're suggesting is that Maggie hike the Pali Trail and distract the guard while I slip into the maintenance shed from the backside?"

"Something like that."

"I don't suppose you would have a weapon of some kind?"

"Do Hawaiian girls dance the hula?" She grinned. She reached into her bag and produced a snub-nosed .38. "A girl living alone can't be too careful these days."

"We really appreciate this," I said, "but aren't you afraid of these guys?"

"I probably should be, but I love my island home, and I hate this thing that is dividing my people. We each must do what we can to bring an end to the bitterness."

"By any chance, is there a Radio Shack in Lahaina?"

"Sure is. It's just around the corner from Hilo Hatties."

We parted with hugs all around and good wishes.

When Maggie and I were alone, I took her by the shoulders and looked into those beautiful blue eyes.

"Are you up for this? Because if you're not—"

"Are you kidding? I've always wanted to tell you to take a hike."

Is she special or what?

CHAPTER TWENTY-TWO

As tired as we were, we slept very little. I kept playing our hastily drawn plan over and over in my mind. There were just so many things that could go wrong.

I frankly didn't know if I was physically able to hike three thousand feet straight up the side of a mountain.

We were up before dawn, grabbed a quick breakfast, and hailed a cab to take us to the nearest car rental outlet.

Our next stop was the local Radio Shack. We needed a set of walkie-talkies to stay in touch. My climb would be longer and tougher than Maggie's, and she would certainly reach her destination before me. It was essential that we coordinate our arrival at the wind farm. As the old saying goes, "Timing is everything."

We followed the crude map that Noelani had given us and easily located the turn-off to the Lahaina Pali Trailhead.

Maggie was ready to go. Our plan was to have Maggie distract the guard at the shack so that I could sneak in from behind. To that end, she had dressed in butt-hugging short shorts, a low-cut top that tied just under her boobs leaving her midriff exposed, and her hair was pulled back into a saucy ponytail.

I knew that part of our plan was foolproof.

I certainly was distracted.

I held her close and hated to send her off on this incredible journey, but we both knew that the lives of our friends depended on us.

As I watched her disappear through the kiawe trees to the trailhead, I marveled at what a special woman I had found. I figured that if we could just survive our honeymoon, the rest of our married life would be a breeze.

It was a twenty-minute drive to my trailhead, and I wasted another ten minutes just trying to find the darn thing. It was not clearly marked as the other one. Maybe that's because people aren't supposed to be on it.

I parked just off the gravel road, checked my gear, and headed up the mountain.

A few hundred feet up the trail, I keyed the walkie-talkie to make sure I could reach Maggie.

"Maggie, can you hear me?"

"Loud and clear. Oh, Walt, it's so beautiful up here. I had no idea. I can see all the way back to Lahaina and across the channel. Lanai is just breathtaking."

"Speaking of breathtaking, how's the climb?"

"Not too bad, really. A few steep spots like Noelani said, but I'll be okay."

"I'll check back with you in a half hour or so. You call if you need me."

After another fifteen minutes climb, I saw what Maggie was talking about. The trail rose so steeply that I could see the whole western coast of the island in one direction, and across the valley, the blue waters of Kahului Harbor glistened in the sun. The glorious vista before me momentarily diverted my attention from the grim task that lay ahead.

I kept at a steady pace, resting only briefly to catch my breath and marvel at the scene that continued to unfold as I climbed higher and higher. I checked on Maggie regularly as I had promised, and with each communication, I noticed that she was barely panting while I found it difficult to even talk through my wheezing and gasping for air.

When Noelani said the trail was "straight up the mountain," she wasn't kidding. I'm no math wizard, but I figured that the angle of ascent varied between forty and sixty degrees—ninety, of course, being straight up.

My breathing was labored, and my thighs and calves were screaming at me. I was beginning to wonder if there would be enough left of me to confront the bad guys if I even made it to the top.

After an hour and a half of this torture, the trail peaked over a little rise, and in the distance I saw the tips of the huge windmills. The trail leveled off at this point, and seeing my goal within reach, I felt a surge of new energy.

For someone younger, this might be considered a "second wind," but I had used that up long before. This was probably my fourth or fifth wind.

I silently wondered how many winds I had left.

The trail I was on didn't actually lead to the wind farm, so I had to abandon the trail and venture through the brush to reach our objective. I crouched a few hundred yards behind the maintenance shed and keyed Maggie.

"Okay, I made it. Where are you?"

"I'm at the intersection where the Pali Trail crosses the service road. It will probably take me ten minutes to climb to the wind farm."

"Great. Leave your mike open so I can hear what's happening on your end. When I know you've made contact, I'll slip in the back. You be careful!"

I inched closer to the shed, being careful to stay low and out of sight. I stopped when I figured the final distance would take only a few minutes.

Presently, I heard a gruff voice over the walkie-talkie.

"Hey, lady! You're not supposed to be up here. Didn't you see the signs on the trail?"

"Oh my goodness, no. I was so intrigued by those huge windmills. I just had to get a closer look. Big, powerful things like that really turn me on."

Wow! If that didn't get his attention, he was either gay or dead.

"Well, uh, I don't think it's a good idea to—"

"Oh, and silly me. I ran out of water, and I'm really thirsty. If you have something cold to drink up there, I could be *really* grateful."

I could just imagine her standing there, her hand coyly perched on her hip just above those long, shapely legs.

"Well, maybe for just a minute."

She had him!

I took off at a run and reached the shed door while they were a hundred feet away.

The thing we didn't know for sure was whether the guard was alone. The snub-nosed .38 was at the ready, and I held my breath as I slipped in the door.

It was a good-sized shed, maybe twenty-four by forty feet, and the walls were lined with workbenches and toolboxes. There was a lone chair in the corner, and bound to it hand and foot was one Mary Murphy.

Willie was nowhere in sight.

A large piece of duct tape covered Mary's mouth.

I really couldn't blame the guard for that. It had been something I had considered doing myself in weaker moments.

Mary's eyes lit up like a Christmas tree when she saw me. I put my finger to my lips and slipped behind the door. I heard footsteps approaching the shed and Maggie's sultry voice.

"I'll bet you get really lonesome up here all by yourself."

"Yeah, I do," the guard replied as he stepped in the door.

"Well, guess what, dirtbag?" Maggie growled. "You're not alone anymore."

I stepped from behind the door, and the guard froze, staring into the muzzle of the .38.

"Just put your hands in the air and no one will get hurt," I said. "Maggie, take care of Mary." I motioned the guard to the other side of the shed, and Maggie set Mary free.

Mary leaped from the chair and grabbed the guard by the throat.

"Sorry to make you out as a liar, Mr. Walt, 'cause somebody's sure as hell gonna get hurt." And with a punch that would have made George Foreman proud, she walloped the guard in the solar plexus, bending him double. "That'll teach you to mess with Mary Murphy."

"Mary, are you all right?" I knew the answer, but I had to ask.

"I'm a lot better now," she said, rubbing her sore knuckles.

"Where's Willie?"

"Some guy came and took him a couple of hours ago, but I don't know where. But I'll bet this creep knows."

The guard shrunk back into the corner as Mary approached.

"Well, how about it?" I said, turning to the guard. "Where have they taken our friend?"

"I tell you nothing!" he hissed.

I motioned to the chair with the revolver. "Have a seat, and we'll see about that. Maggie, grab that duct tape off the bench, and let's get this guy trussed up."

When the guard was securely bound, I tried again. "Look, buddy, the Kalakoas are dead, your precious artifacts are safely hidden from the world, and we've got you dead to rights. Let's just put an end to all this right now. All we want is the safe return of our friend."

"There will be no end until our kingdom is restored and the land is returned to the Hawaiian people. Many will die, but it is the price of freedom. I tell you nothing."

I looked at Mary and Maggie for suggestions. Interrogation was obviously not my strong suit.

Mary didn't hesitate. "Mr. Walt, why don't you and Maggie step outside for a breath of fresh air? It's getting kind of stuffy in here. Let me have a chat with our friend here."

I wasn't sure that was a good idea, but Maggie grabbed me by the arm and pushed me toward the door.

All was quiet for maybe five minutes, then—

"*Yeow!*"

More silence, then again—

"*Yeow!* No more please!"

The door opened, and Mary stepped out with a knowing smile on her face.

"I think the dude is ready to talk to you now."

I wasn't sure I wanted to know, but I asked anyway.

"What in the world did you do to that guy?"

"All you gotta do is put a pair of pliers to a guy's testicles and he'll tell you anything you want to know."

Involuntarily, Mr. Winkie and the boys recoiled in horror.

"Yeah, I can see how that would work."

When I approached the guard, he was much more cooperative.

"So where have they taken our friend?"

"To the cane fields, just past Puunene." He looked at the clock on the wall. "In thirty minutes your dark friend will be brown sugar."

"What's this idiot talking about?" Mary moved toward the guard with pliers at the ready. "Let me have another shot at him."

"The cane burn. They're burning the cane fields for harvesting. They're going to burn Willie alive! And we only have a half hour to stop them."

"There's a truck outside," Maggie volunteered. "I'll bet this guy's got the keys in his pocket."

"He does, but that's not going to do you any good," said a voice behind us. "Now put down that gun."

We turned and found ourselves staring into the barrel of a twelve-gauge shotgun.

"Now put down that gun and untie my friend. Looks like we've got more kindling for our fire."

I should have realized that there would be more than one guard at the Keheawa wind farm.

I knelt down to lay the .38 on the floor and looked past our captor just in time to see a figure running full speed toward the shed. Recognizing our friend, I yelled to Mary and Maggie, "Hit the floor! Now!"

Liho came barreling through the door and hit the gunman squarely in the back. The shotgun discharged harmlessly into the air then flew from his hands as he hit the floor. Liho flipped the guy onto his back and drove his massive fist into his face.

"What kind of man threatens a woman and child? You will not threaten my family again!"

The second punch put the guy's lights out.

"Liho, they've got Willie in a cane field near a place called Puunene. They're going to burn him. Do you know where that is?"

"It's about fifteen or twenty minutes from here."

"Then we'd better hurry or Willie's toast!"

We hog-tied the second guard and pulled the truck keys from the first guard's pocket.

"I'll drive," Liho said. "I know the fastest way there, and you're not going to want to do what I have to do."

"What's that?"

"Crash the gate at the bottom of the hill."

Thankfully the pickup was an extended cab, and Mary and Maggie piled into the back. I took shotgun.

We barreled down the hill at an alarming speed, and as we approached the locked gate, a guard stood in the road frantically waving his arms.

"Hold on!" Liho said.

At the last minute the guard jumped to the side, and we smashed through the gate just like you see in the movies. I glanced back just in time to see the angry guard give us the finger.

I'm guessing it was a Hawaiian finger, but the translation came through loud and clear.

As we rolled past the Maui Ocean Center, I looked at my watch.

In fifteen minutes, the cane field would be a burning inferno.

Liho hung a right at the Walmart, and we sped toward the old sugar mill—only three minutes left.

"We have normal trade winds today, blowing from east to west," Liho said, "so they'll start the fire on the east side."

We were coming from the west.

As we approached the field, a wisp of smoke rose on the far side.

"Oh crap! We're too late."

I remembered what Harry Chinn had said: "It would only take fifteen minutes to engulf the whole field."

"He has to be in there somewhere," I said. "Let's drive into the middle of the field. We have to find him."

"We're not going to do it in this thing," Liho said. "The cane's too thick. We need a dozer."

"What about that one?" I yelled, pointing to a big Cat that had just finished clearing the fire break around the field. "Can you drive it?"

"I worked in the fields when I was a kid, and I saw my uncle operate one. I hope I can remember."

"It's like riding a bike," I said. "Once you learn, you never forget."

Liho pulled up beside the dozer and hopped into the cab.

I turned to Maggie. "Call Harry Chinn. Get him out here."

I hopped into the cab with Liho, who by this time had the big diesel engine belching smoke.

My heart sank as I looked out over the field.

Forty acres is huge, and to my dismay, I saw that the cane stalks were eight to ten feet tall. From our vantage point in the cab, we could only see a few feet ahead.

I pointed to the blade. "How high will that thing go?"

"Maybe ten feet."

I climbed onto the blade and shouted back, "Take her up as high as she'll go and head for the middle of the field."

The blade lifted into the air, Liho gunned the engine, and we were off.

I could see the flames eating away at the field on the far side. We had maybe five minutes before we would be engulfed in the fiery conflagration. We plowed ahead, but all that I could see was cane.

Then fifty feet ahead, I saw an iron fence post that had been driven into the ground, and bound to it was my friend Willie.

I pointed in the direction of the post, and Liho swung the big machine around.

The flames were close enough that I could feel the searing heat as I jumped from the blade to free my friend. I had my pocketknife ready to cut loose his bindings, but a feeling of dread swept over me when I saw that he was bound with wire.

I had no wire cutters or pliers, and I stood helplessly watching the advancing flames.

At that moment, a small gecko, fleeing the flaming inferno, crawled onto the dozer's blade. He looked at me, and he looked at Willie; then he leaped into the fence post and disappeared.

Okay, I thought, *if I can't get Willie off the post, then we'll just have to take the whole thing.*

I motioned for Liho to bring the blade flush with the post then push gently. The post leaned forward in the soft ground. Liho backed off, and I pulled Willie and the post upright. The post wiggled back and forth, and I hoped it was loose enough because the fire was advancing fast.

I climbed onto the top of the blade into a sitting position and wrapped my arms and legs around the post and Willie's torso. I motioned for Liho to lift the blade, and I hung on for dear life.

At first the post remained stubbornly in the ground, but Liho inched the blade forward just enough to break it loose, and the blade lifted skyward with me holding Willie and the post tightly in my arms.

The back of the dozer left the clearing just as the flames broke through. The dozer slowly plowed ahead, but the flames were moving faster.

Just as the burning cane was about to overtake the big Cat, a burst of water nearly blew me off the blade.

A huge pumper truck used for irrigation had been pressed into service and retarded the advancing flames just long enough for us to reach the edge of the field.

I can only imagine the shock of the onlookers who had gathered to watch the spectacle, when the huge dozer burst through the smoking cane carrying a white guy on the blade who was clutching a black man on a stick.

It's something you don't see every day.

After Willie was cut free, we found Maggie and Mary, and we fell into each other's arms.

We hugged and we cried and we hugged again.

When it's all said and done, I'll bet this will be a honeymoon that none of us will ever forget.

Detective Harry Chinn arrived minutes after our harrowing escape from Pele's fiery cauldron. He listened in utter disbelief as we recounted the improbable rescue of our two friends.

With our testimony, the men responsible for our abduction were captured and remained in custody, but the battle of ideologies was far from over.

Throughout history, men have fought one another and given their lives to protect their basic rights and freedoms.

These men were labeled revolutionaries, terrorists, martyrs, or heroes, depending on your point of view.

And somehow it seems that one significant entity has been excluded from this ongoing saga of mankind. That entity is Lady Justice.

There is no greater paradox than the history of our own United States.

The brave settlers of the New World fought to free themselves from the tyranny of the British Empire, yet these same revolutionaries took the land and freedom from the Native Americans, who were branded as "vicious savages" for fighting to protect their way of life.

Heroes or savages?

And as if to validate the old saying, "History repeats itself," men sailed across the Pacific to a small chain of islands and in the course of a hundred years took the land, the government, the religion, and the way of life from the indigenous population.

Where is the justice in all this?

That is the question being asked still today by some who seek the return of their land and the restoration of their government.

Heroes or terrorists?

I guess it depends on your point of view.

There is an old saying, "Never judge a man until you've walked a mile in his shoes."

With that in mind, I find it difficult to condemn those who seek justice and restitution, but at the same time, there is truth to the wise words of my old friend Nathan: "You can't un-ring a bell."

What's done is done, and sometimes the best that that can be done is to get the lady with the blindfold involved and hope that justice prevails for the generations to come.

We were thankful that our remaining days in paradise were free from murder, mayhem, and evil deeds.

We did all the wonderful stuff that tourists do. We spent a day at the Maui Ocean Center, explored the beautiful Iao Valley, and soaked up the warm tropical sun on the sandy beach.

One evening, as we strolled along Front Street in Lahaina, I was drawn into one of the little souvenir shops. There were both T-shirts and bumper stickers proudly proclaiming, "I got lei'd in Maui."

I bought two of each.

Later that evening I asked Noelani about the history of the Hawaiian lei. She told me that the lei had been a part of the Polynesian culture beginning with the first voyagers who sailed to the islands. Leis were symbols of love, of a spiritual meaning or connection, of healing, and of respect. The *maile lei* was perhaps the most significant. Among other sacred uses, it was used to signify a peace agreement between opposing chiefs.

Reflecting later on our conversation, I thought how wonderful it would be if somehow Lady Justice could bring the lei of peace to the leaders of the Hawaiian people, to ensure that the history and culture of their people would be preserved and passed on to future generations.

The significance of the double entendre in the bumper sticker was certainly not lost on me.

Maggie and I had chosen this place out of all of the beautiful places in the world to exchange our wedding vows, and we were not disappointed. In years to come, as we go about our life back on the mainland, we will remember these weeks in paradise.

We will remember standing on the bridge over the lagoon at the Coco Palms, where our two lives became one.

We will remember all of the beautiful beaches and mountains.

But most of all, we will remember the beautiful people who will always remain our friends: Jimmy on Oahu; Sammy and Uncle Larry on Kauai; Liho, Noelani, Nathan, and even Detective Chinn on Maui.

Noelani told me that over the years, as the tourist industry blossomed, "Boat Day" became a tradition on Oahu. Lei vendors would line the pier at Aloha Tower to welcome visitors to the island and locals back home. It is said that departing visitors would throw their lei into the sea as the ship passed Diamond Head, in hopes that, like the lei, they would return to the islands again someday.

As our plane taxied down the runway and lifted into the sky, I saw the great dormant volcano Haleakala standing like a sentinel, a silent witness, to both the past and the future of this beautiful island, and I felt the connection that Maggie and I would always have with this magnificent mountain.

In my mind's eye, I removed the flower lei from around my neck and cast it onto the craggy peaks of the summit, knowing that someday we too would return.

ABOUT THE AUTHOR

At age sixty-six, Robert Thornhill wrote his first two mystery/comedy novels, *Lady Justice Takes A C.R.A.P.* and *Lady Justice and the Lost Tapes.*

This third novel in the Lady Justice series, *Lady Justice Gets Lei'd*, has special meaning for the author.

Robert and his wife, Peg, like Walt and Maggie, were married in Hawaii and recreated Elvis's marriage ceremony in *Blue Hawaii.*

Robert and Peg lived on the island of Maui for five years.

Robert has also written the Rainbow Road series of children's chapter books.

Robert holds a master's in psychology, but his wit and insight come from his varied occupations, including thirty years as a real estate broker.

He lives with his wife, Peg, in Independence, Missouri.

For more information, go to
www.BooksByBob.com

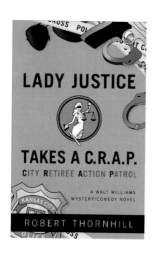

This is where it all began.

See how sixty-five-year-old Walter Williams became a cop and started the City Retiree Action Patrol.

Meet Maggie, Willie, Mary, and the professor, Walt's sidekicks in all of the Lady Justice novels.

Laugh out loud as Walt and his band of senior scrappers capture the Realtor Rapist and take down the Russian Mob.

For more information, go to www.BooksByBob.com